Kingdom Come

DANIELLE M. ORSINO

KINGDOM COME

Birth of the Fae Book 4

4 Horsemen
Publications, Inc.

From Kingdom Come
Birth of the Fae: Vol 1 Book 4
Copyright © 2021 Danielle M. Orsino. All rights reserved.

4 Horsemen
Publications, Inc.

4 Horsemen Publications, Inc.
1497 Main St. Suite 169
Dunedin, FL 34698
4horsemenpublications.com
info@4horsemenpublications.com

Cover by Horsemen Publications, Inc.
Typesetting by Michelle Cline
Editor S. L. Vargas

Cover model "Jarvok": George Tsambis-Weisner
Map is illustrated by Daniel Hasenbos–he goes by Daniels Maps
Photo : Julia Juliati
Makeup and Hair: Denise M. Apostle
Aurora's Premonition Concept: Danielle M. Orsino
Aurora's Premonition illustration: PandiiVan

All rights to the work within are reserved to the author and publisher. No part of this publication may be reproduced, stored in a retrieval system, or transmitted in any form or by any means, electronic, mechanical, photocopying, recording, scanning, or otherwise, except as permitted under Section 107 or 108 of the 1976 International Copyright Act, without prior written permission except in brief quotations embodied in critical articles and reviews. Please contact either the Publisher or Author to gain permission.

This book is meant as a reference guide. All characters, organizations, and events portrayed in this novel are either products of the author's imagination or are used fictitiously. All brands, quotes, and cited work respectfully belong to the original rights holders and bear no affiliation to the authors or publisher.

Library of Congress Control Number: 2022931338

Print ISBN: 978-1-64450-528-1
eBook ISBN: 978-1-64450-527-4
Audio ISBN: 978-1-64450-526-7

Table of Contents

Prologue xv
Chapter One: A Change Will Do
    Who Good? 1
Chapter Two: Silence Says Everything 13
Chapter Three: A Call to Action 21
Chapter Four: A Bigger Issue 37
Chapter Five: A Fae in the Oven 43
Chapter Six: Wipe the Smile Off Your Face . 51
Chapter Seven: And So It Begins............. 58
Chapter Eight: In Search Of................. 64
Chapter Nine: I Knew Him.................... 70
Chapter Ten: A Fae Walked In................ 79
Chapter Eleven: One Final Request......... 87
Chapter Twelve: Into the Woods 92
Chapter Thirteen: Partners in Crime 101
Chapter Fourteen: The Jesus Factor 106
Chapter Fifteen: The Mountain Comes
    to the Fae................................ 111
Chapter Sixteen: Is That All There Is?..... 115
Chapter Seventeen: One Last Speech 122
Chapter Eighteen: Nerves 131

CHAPTER NINETEEN: ALL MY LOATH AND
　　BLIGHT UPON YOU 134
CHAPTER TWENTY: HELP ME TO HELP YOU TO
　　HELP ME.... 148
CHAPTER TWENTY-ONE: DREAM WARRIORS ...158
CHAPTER TWENTY-TWO: RESPONSIBILITY 171
CHAPTER TWENTY-THREE: BLOSSOMS AND TEA 174
CHAPTER TWENTY-FOUR: HEAVY IS THE
　　HEART THAT WEARS THE CROWN 181
CHAPTER TWENTY-FIVE: THREE BISHOPS,
　　A QUEEN AND A MOTHER 190
CHAPTER TWENTY-SIX: OPPORTUNITY
　　KNOCKS.....................................195
CHAPTER TWENTY-SEVEN: IT'S JUST MY HEART
　　THAT HURTS 198
CHAPTER TWENTY-EIGHT: IT'S NOT NICE
　　TO UPSET MOTHER NATURE 202
CHAPTER TWENTY-NINE: NO PLACE FOR
　　LITTLE ONES............................. 207
CHAPTER THIRTY: AN EMPATH'S WORK 213
CHAPTER THIRTY-ONE: A FRIEND IN NEED IS A
　　FRIEND INDEED...........................219
CHAPTER THIRTY-TWO: AN OATH REALIZED ...225
CHAPTER THIRTY-THREE: REVENGE 233

Dedication

Life can be lonely, but you are never alone; through books you can travel and escape. I am honored you have picked up this passport into a new world. Consider me your tour guide. Come get lost for a bit and allow me to show you a place where magic, love, wonder, and fantasy exist. Together we will ride a dragon, and maybe when you leave the Veil, you will have made some new friends and recognized the magic inside you.

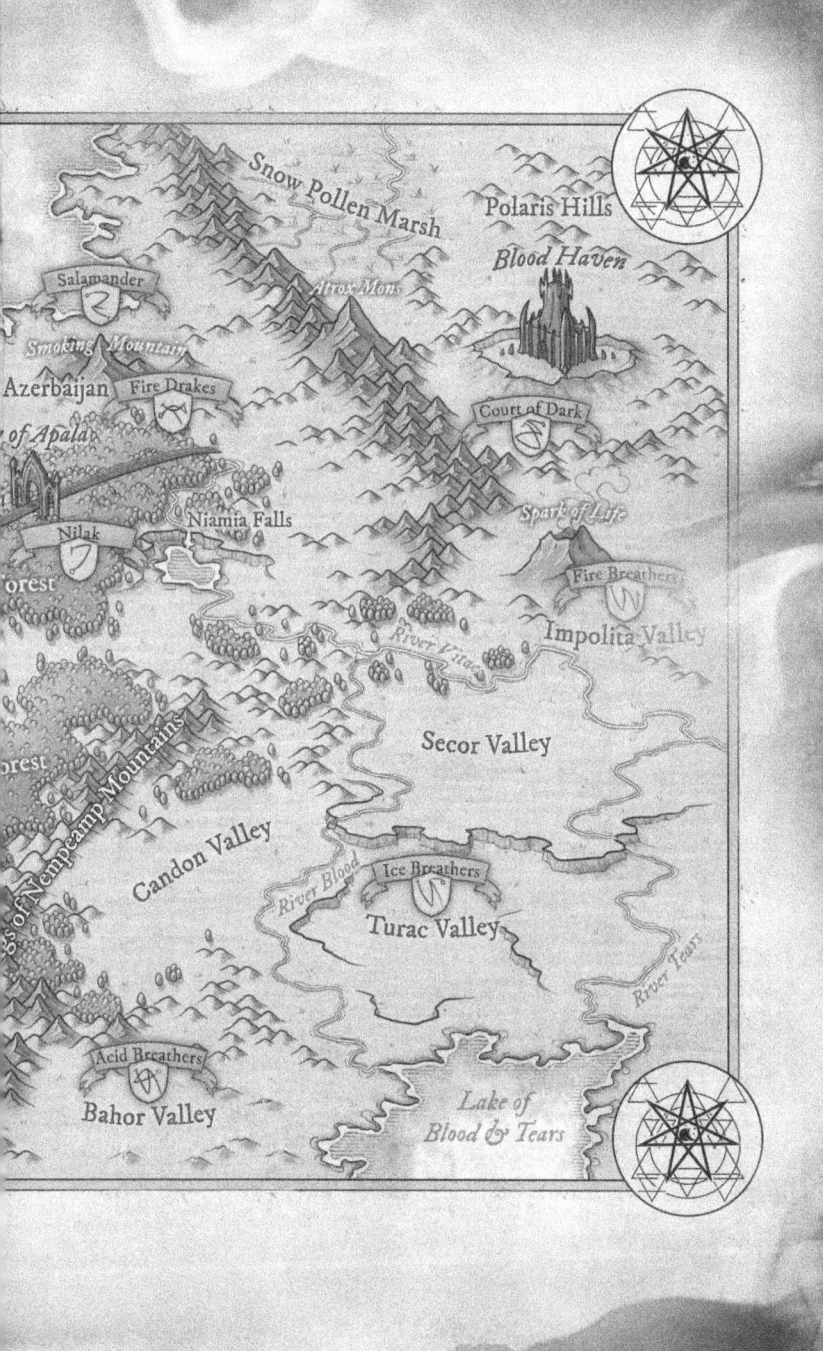

Acknowledgements

PMD

Carlos and Penelope: My little luvs

The 4Horsemen

Denise Apostle: Thank you for being a creative collaborator and helping me to bring these characters to life with your wonderful makeup and talent.

Morris Freeman

And to all my Fae friends: Thank you for taking this journey with me.

Prologue

Ah, the Veil. The Court of Light, to be precise. I have been observing the Fae for so very long now. They are no threat to me; I find them amusing. Especially that last squabble Jarvok and Aurora had. I mean, a vapor dragon. I am still fanboying over that one. Well done, Jarvok!

I watched this group of cast-offs rebuild themselves after the Creator locked them out of the Shining Kingdom so long ago. They earned my respect at first—rebuilding and redefining who they were. That is until I realized they did all this not to spite their almighty, but despite him. They can act like such simpletons.

Aurora has forgiven and evolved—good for her. It seems the queen has found common ground with the Dark Fae king. Yes, they are in love… Could you just die! It's so sweet. Excuse me while I grab my airsickness bag. Yet, she continues to ignore the signs that all is not well in the Veil. Her bishops grow distant but, she still trusts them. Sure, when has trusting a band of scheming men ever not worked out for a woman in power?

The Fae are still so concerned with their daddy. They don't see how their issues sully everything they do. Even now when they have peace after a long, bloody war. They should be celebrating, but instead of being happy, they are stuck in their feelings. The bishops are upset with their queen and her choice to welcome the Dark Fae into the fold. Like the bishops, some Light Fae are holding fast to their old Virtue beliefs sowing seeds of discord. Worrying about what dear ol' dad would think—it makes me sick.

The Fae born of the Earth aren't much better; pitiful, actually. They do not know what suffering is. They prick their fingers on a thorn bush and cry. Pockets of these younger Fae feel the war was not theirs to win or lose. They can't grasp the bigger picture but will jump onto a cause if their friends tell them to.

The older, bitter Fae are leading the younger ones, whipping them up into a frenzy, causing a rebellion. The insurgents are becoming emboldened as they listen to propaganda about how their beloved queen is defaming the sacrifices of the fallen Fae who gave their light for the war. A war those Earthborn Fae have no connection to. But fear is a motivator. If the queen lies with the king, she may put the Dark Fae above the Light Fae. It's all a manipulation. Simpletons.

Do I care? No, I do not. While these Fae prance about, neglecting the humans who still worship them as their pantheon of gods and goddesses, droughts are more prevalent, crops are ruined, and illnesses run rampant. Soon the old religion will pass on—making it easier for me to take center stage, where I belong.

It's the usual trope: one conversation, and much of this could have been avoided. Queen Aurora should have told King Jarvok about the mounting rebellion their unification was causing. But she knows the Dark Fae king rules

Prologue

with a Kyanite fist. He would put a swift end to the tension bubbling under the surface. And rightfully so. I always appreciated his take-no-prisoners attitude, even when he was a Power Brigade Angel. Aurora believes she can handle this on her own, or perhaps she naively hopes it will simply work itself out. I think she doesn't trust her lover as much as she says she does, for deep down she knows he is the better ruler.

They are all pawns in this game, and I should know; I am the one playing across from the Creator. I have been waiting to see how I can use them to my advantage, and my persistence is about to pay off. If patience is a virtue, then knowledge is power. I have both. Let's see how our little lovebirds are doing. Something tells me there is a snake among them, and no, it's not me.

Chapter One:
A Change Will Do Who Good?

King Jarvok, leader of the Dark Fae, called the meeting of the High Council Guard into session. His two lieutenants, Zion and Asa, stood tall and silent at his side, ready to serve.

"I have asked you all here today to inform you of the decisions I have made regarding the blending of our court with the Light Fae. I am due to deliver details of my reorganization of the Court of Dark to Queen Aurora by the full moon. Therefore, I wanted you to be aware of the changes that will befall us once the unification ceremony takes place."

The members of the High Council Guard had very different reactions to the king's declaration. Yagora and Pria exchanged uneasy glances. Azrael and Ezekiel leaned forward, hanging on their king's every word. Jonah's head drooped forward, his eyes half closed and shot up just before his chin hit his chest. Zion and Asa stayed put at the head of the obsidian crystal table. Jarvok paced.

Los, a small dragon with the rare ability to blend into his surroundings like a chameleon, was perched at the observation window, trying to stay out of the way. His pink tongue lolled out of his mouth as it always did. His large, dark eyes focused on the Dark Fae king as he methodically paced. The dragon was aware of the gravity of the situation.

Holly, a black mink and Lady Zarya's Familiar, was snuggled around the neck of the Court of Dark's Oracle. The two were present to lend any support should their king need it. Dragor, King Jarvok's dragon companion and leader of the Draconian Faction, snored, sharing Jonah's lack of enthusiasm for the meeting.

Jarvok's union with Queen Aurora of the Court of Light was not planned. The courts had been embroiled in a long, drawn-out civil war for close to a millennium. A treaty was eventually reached, and the two sides saw a halt in fighting. Until Queen Mary I of England reneged on a reproduction contract with the Court of Light. This culminated in Awynn, a bishop from the Court of Light, sacrificing himself to save Jarvok in a tumultuous standoff between the two sides.

Aurora and Jarvok had had a knockdown, drag-out battle. Jarvok smiled at the memory. *If the others only knew that the battle would have led to us both meeting our Oblivion if not for the ghosts of the past.* A simple, kind gesture from long ago had broken their anger in the heat of battle; the two monarchs learned they had been guiding each other in many ways. Aurora observed that if they had been assisting each other without knowing it, imagine what they could do if they actively tried to help one another. But what started as unification for survival was now about blending the two courts because they wanted to be together, not because they were forced to. Love had won over hate.

What a change from the day a contorted feather floated across my face—when I woke up with no name on an abandoned beach as a broken Power Angel. He was now King Jarvok, leader of the Dark Fae, betrothed to Queen Aurora of the Court of Light—a former Virtue Angel, of all things. He glanced up at the several sets of eyes fixated on him. Holly cleared her throat, and Jarvok continued to speak, his commanding voice booming.

"I will be keeping Blood Haven as home to the Weepers and as our main training facility. Therefore, I will need a Fae to oversee it," Jarvok said as he paced the room. "Most of the dragons will stay here. Dragor, you will accompany me, of course, and Los too."

The black dragon snorted, lifting one eyelid. He was going to let Jarvok enjoy his air of authority. They were connected at the hip and heart; wherever one went, the other followed.

Los chortled in excitement, not that there was ever doubt he would be going with Jarvok. Los was as close to a son as any dragon could be.

Jarvok turned his attention to Zion. "Lieutenant Zion, if Queen Aurora and I do not produce an heir to the new Court of the Fae, I am petitioning you be the heir to the throne."

The room gasped, all turning to stare at the lieutenant.

"My liege?" Zion's head jerked back. "I thought I was to remain here—"

Jarvok raised his hand to silence his lieutenant. "You are my second-in-command. We are unsure if Aurora can reproduce, so it would be fair my second be the heir, representing the Court of Dark to keep the courts balanced. You will accompany me to the Court of Light and learn to rule. Should we produce a successor, you will be a most trusted advisor both militarily and in the old ways of the Power Brigade. You will hold a highly respected position."

Jarvok met Zion's gaze. He could sense the Fae was disappointed—that Zion would prefer to watch over Blood Haven, protecting it. But this was a way for Jarvok to tell Zion how much he trusted him, even if his second could not see it yet.

"It would be my honor," Zion finally said, straightening.

Jarvok nodded. "That leaves the business of Blood Haven and who will remain here as its custodian."

Pria and Yagora held hands under the table. Jarvok caught their gesture out of the corner of his eye, but he swung his gaze in the opposite direction.

Azrael exhaled, watching Yagora and Pria. After the events of the dragon tournament, he was not at all pleased with them, but now was not the time to address it.

"Lieutenant Asa, you will accompany me to the Court of Light for the unification ceremony, but afterward, you will return here as mistress of Blood Haven," Jarvok announced.

"What?" Pria whispered in Yagora's ear, dropping her hand under the table.

"*Her?*" Yagora asked aloud.

"How could he?" Pria said under her breath.

Azrael covered his smile. He was enjoying Pria and Yagora's displeasure.

Yagora slammed her hands on the table, her white and black hair falling forward. She stood, and her arms shook as she hit the table again, unable to handle Pria's disappointment. "She is not worthy, my liege, nor is she strong enough! Let me face her in the ring of combat! I will show you she is not the Fae to lead Blood Haven." Her nostrils flared.

Asa remained silent. Zion put his forearm across her middle, blocking her and glanced at Asa, shaking his head.

Although Jarvok was stoic, both Los and Dragor knew it was not a good sign. The dragons' ear feathers twitched in their own wordless communication.

Jarvok snuffed out the flame of a candle with his hand and licked his lips, tasting the fear that permeated the air. His Black Kyanite boots were heavy on the obsidian floor, yet he moved with boneless grace toward Yagora. "You dare to question me?" His voice was controlled like a slow-burning fire, chewing up kindling before it became a raging inferno.

Yagora's eyes remained on Asa as the king closed the distance between them. He raised his chin, his imposing figure impossible to ignore. Yagora finally looked up, her eyes meeting Jarvok's amber gaze, but she could not hold his stare. "You do not seem to have much to say now, Yagora," he said. "Perhaps it is because you do not think for yourself. It is why I did not choose you. You are a follower, not a leader. Step aside."

Yagora did as she was told.

Behind her was the puppet master. Pria glanced up at her king, but she too could not hold his gaze.

"Ah, the brains behind the operation. You poked the troll to get it to roar. Do you think me stupid, Pria? Did you assume I was not aware of the Fae you blended with to gain intel? The relationship you formed with Yagora to ice out Asa, hoping to make her yearn for your friendship, so she would divulge information about her king? All your doomed schemes? Do you really think I was not privy to them? My dear, I am not king of the Court of Dark because I am naive. In one sense, I can almost applaud your cunning. It was one of the reasons I have kept you around so long, but it is why you have come so very close to Oblivion. Therefore..." Jarvok unsheathed his Elestial Blade in one fluid motion. The aura-charged weapon lit the room up in a warm white glow, and he slashed Pria across her face, opening an ugly gash on her right cheek. She dropped and grabbed for her face as blue blood leaked between her fingers.

Jarvok bent down and grabbed a fistful of her teal hair. As he pulled her head back, a low whisper came from the back of his throat. "That is a reminder, Pria. Incite my anger again, and next time it will be your neck my blade cuts through. Consider this your final warning. Now take your seat and let us finish this." He released her with a push.

Pria found her way to her feet and bowed to her king. Yagora reached out to help her, but Pria shrugged her off. King Jarvok returned to the matters at hand as if nothing had transpired. "As I was saying, Lieutenant Asa will be mistress of Blood Haven. She will be in command of the Weepers and their training. I will disband the High Council Guard. Some of you will remain here under her command, while others will accompany me and Lieutenant Zion to the Court of Fae to act as advisors. You will be part of a new Council composed of representatives from both courts. I will request the best of the Illuminasqua train with a handpicked group of our fiercest warriors to make up a mixed fighting force. I believe it is best for everyone

A Change Will Do Who Good?

if the Weepers remain separate from the Light Fae. They are too unpredictable. In the name of peace, let's not invite trouble. They do best when we keep them on routine." He glared around the room, daring any Fae to speak. The group was silent. Jonah tugged at his ear. Yagora quietly lent comfort to Pria, who held her cheek. Jarvok surveyed the table, stoic yet mindful. "Any comments?"

The table remained silent. Pria's cheek had stopped bleeding. Azrael sat tall. Yagora ceased her attempts to help Pria. Ezekiel sharpened a small blade.

Dragor huffed, and the scent of sulfur from his flint rock–covered back teeth wafted throughout the room. His long tail flicked, fanning the flames, so to speak. It seemed Dragor had something to say.

Holly jumped down from the table to speak with him. The two exchanged sounds and grunts. "Are you sure you want me to ask this in front of everyone?" she asked, her voice floating up to those seated at the table. The dragon bobbed his head.

"Ask me, Dragor," Jarvok said, catching wind of the conversation. He could understand his dragon perfectly, but Dragor was looking to make a point by involving the mink, letting the king know the Shadow Realm was aware of the issue.

Holly scurried back to the table and stood in the middle of the table, holding court, facing the king. "Dragor is concerned about how some of the Draconian Faction members will feel about living with the Light Fae, especially the Ice-Breathers. The Battle of Secor Valley is still a sore subject, King Jarvok. They want to know their sacred ways will be honored. Can you speak with the queen regarding this before you ask the Ice-Breathers to follow you?"

Jarvok strode up to the leader of the Draconian Faction, bowing his head. "I have not forgotten what happened at the Battle of Secor Valley. I understand the Ice-Breathers have not either. I think it is best the Ice-Breathers stay here at Blood Haven with Yanka and Asa. I do agree we need some kind of acknowledgment regarding the travesty that transpired, and see the sacred ways are protected under a treaty. I will make sure this is addressed in the meeting. You should accompany me. Once we have come to a resolution, they can follow us to the Court of Light."

Dragor rose and curved his long, serpentine neck in a display of respect.

The king turned to the mink. "Thank you, Holly." She gave him a slow blink and returned to Lady Zarya, who stroked her Familiar for a job well done.

Lady Zarya spoke up next. "King Jarvok, will you be living in the Court of Light's palace or constructing a new one?"

The room's attention zeroed in on him. "I am not sure. We have not discussed living arrangements. Considering the Veil, I really do not know what the best option is." Jarvok's voice betrayed his lack of confidence in the process.

"And what of the Veil?" Azrael asked. "Will you share with the queen the fact that you created two layers of it and reveal how the Court of Dark travels through them?"

Ezekiel paused his sharpening.

Jarvok pulled at the hairs on the back of his neck. He wanted to be open with his new love, but his head said not to. It was the Court of Dark's top defense. "No, I will not share that piece of information with the Court of Light. I feel it is in our best interests to keep it off the table." Everyone seemed to breathe a sigh of relief. Jarvok glanced at Lady Zarya, who gave a subtle chin tilt as if to reassure him of his decision.

Azrael stroked his cheek, still worried about the secrecy of their Veil within a Veil. "No disrespect, my liege, but Queen Aurora has never mentioned to you that the Light Fae cannot see Blood Haven from the Smoking Mountain?"

Lady Zarya placed a hand on Azrael's shoulder. "Azrael, the Smoking Mountain was home to the Fire Drakes. Most of the faction died soon after Lady Kit at the Battle of the Red Sea. Bishop Awynn was the last of them, and he went into his training as a bishop when he was a little one. The peak of the Smoking Mountain has been abandoned since the Fire Drakes met their Oblivion."

Azrael shook his head, patting Zarya's hand. "There are still other vantage points. How have the Light Fae not noticed this?"

Jarvok sighed. "Azrael, the next best place to spot Blood Haven is by the Niamia Falls or close to our side of the Bridge of Oroki. Aurora would not violate the treaty by crossing into our territory. I have no intention of telling Aurora about our Veil. She crafted her Veil, and we—well, *improved* upon it. Does that put your mind at ease?"

Azrael nodded. He had been Archangel Michael's apprentice and working around nothing but weaponry for so long had made him paranoid.

"Lady Zarya, you, Holly, and my lieutenants will accompany me to the Court of Light for the logistical meeting on the full moon. Jonah and Azrael, I will leave the two of you to oversee training exercises. Zion will give you a list of the last-minute preparations."

Jonah stood. "Yes, my liege."

Jarvok gestured to Zion to open the doors. "Good, this meeting is dismissed."

The High Council Guard filed out. Pria tried to linger behind with Yagora, but Zion grabbed them both by the arms and propelled them out.

Asa was left alone with her king. "My liege, may I speak with you?"

Standing at the observation window, Jarvok hung his head. He was drained from the meeting. So many questions had been raised, and Jarvok was doubting all of it. He needed peace and quiet, rather than a focus on emotions, which Asa liked to discuss. "Lieutenant Asa, is this something we need to do right now?" His voice dripped with exhaustion.

"I need to know: why me?"

Jarvok gave a long, deliberate exhale. "You are the best Fae to oversee this fortress, the Weepers, and of course, the Draconians. You are a fierce warrior, yet you see the emotional composition of a situation. I know you are loyal and ethical."

She glanced down, her eyes darting side to side as if deciding how to configure her next comment. "But for those very reasons, do you not believe it would behoove you to have me at your side in the new kingdom?"

Jarvok was befuddled. He had hoped Asa would see this as a reward for her years by his side, that he valued her, but she seemed to be taking it as a rejection. He cracked his neck to the left; the tension did not dissipate. "Asa, Blood Haven is the very spot where I crashed after Archangel Uriel blew the Wormwood trumpet at me. I was broken in both mind and body. I hoped Oblivion was only seconds away when you and Zion helped to pull me from the depths of the crater. Giving you Blood Haven is my way of saying I am grateful to you. Without you both standing by my side for all these millennia, I do not believe peace between the two courts would be possible. I am giving you the place that ended my life as a Power Angel but birthed my reign as king."

Asa dropped to her knees in the traditional position of humility, digging for something in her armor.

King Jarvok observed her without speaking or moving toward her. She lifted her hand up to her king, and a blue stone gleamed in her palm.

Jarvok furrowed his brow and took the stone from her outstretched hand. "You kept your disc?"

"Yes, my liege. When I saw the Angelite disc in Queen Aurora's crown, and it was revealed you were their Shooting Star, I dug mine up to give to you as tribute. I was going to wait until your unification ceremony, but after what you just said, it feels right to present it to you now."

Jarvok rubbed the blue Angelite disc between his thumb and index finger, the fissure that signified their abandonment from the Shining Kingdom catching on his skin. The Angelite crystal held their Glory from the Shining Kingdom. Each of them had ripped their disc out of their heads once they discovered they had been abandoned. He had done it himself, as had Zion and Asa. The members of the High Council Guard had asked him to do it for them. This small crystal represented their life long ago as Power Angels, and when a Power died, it was given as tribute to their commanding Archangel.

The pain from that time was not as cutting as it had once been. He realized it was due to his kin and his relationship with Aurora. He glanced at his third-in-command.

Asa's gaze stayed on the ground, her forehead bowed. He bit his cheek, trying not to show any emotion. She was special to him, and he was even more confident in his choice. He thought about the times he had been hard on her. Those occasions had been born of his own fear and self-doubt. He had been wrong, so very wrong to treat her like that.

Jarvok recognized he would send Pria to her Oblivion if she messed with Asa again, he could not undo his prior treatment of Asa, but he recognized today how much Pria and Yagora had taunted her over the years. He would not allow it to continue. Asa's heart was far too good.

"Rise, Lieutenant Asa." Jarvok moved his gauntlet up on his left arm, exposing the inside of his left wrist, below his palm. He unsheathed his Elestial Blade, and she backed up as he cut into his skin, marking an oval shape. His skin burned and sizzled, but he placed her disc inside his left wrist, fusing it to himself permanently. She watched as the flesh around the disc seared and hissed. Jarvok never flinched. The skin glowed, and the blade turned blue for a flash and retracted; he turned his arm over to show her. There was her Angelite disc embedded into her king's left wrist. The left side of the body represented feminine energy and receiving energy; by placing her disc on the left, he was telling Asa he accepted her energy, love, and light. There was nothing for her to say. It was the ultimate sign of respect and love.

He met her eyes, and an unspoken admiration passed between them. She dipped from the waist and exited to leave him to his thoughts.

Chapter Two:
Silence Says Everything

Rowan sat across from Queen Aurora. The sun was at its highest point, and the meeting had been due to begin well before this. However, the table was to hold six, and currently it was occupied by only Rowan, the queen, and Theadova. The bishops were nowhere to be found. Queen Aurora huffed and mumbled, pushing her chair back. She stood to pace about the room.

"Your Grace, I believe either your bishops are sending a message of defiance, or we are poor company. And in my case, well ... that is impossible," the champagne fox said.

Theadova nodded. The white deer's golden antlers caught the light. Aurora glanced at him and noticed that the edges of Theadova's antlers were adorned by small green leaves and buds, an indication of his age. After their abandonment, Theadova was one of the first Virtue Angels to use the last of his Glory to take the form of fauna. He was the leader of what was now only a handful of White Deer in the Aubane Faction. She frowned. It seemed like only yesterday he was her companion when she set out to meet the primitive humans for the first time, when they both discovered the power of worship. *How very long ago*, she thought. Back then, she was such a young queen, still unsure of what it meant to lead.

She glanced back at the white stag, and the image in her mind of Theadova with flowers on his mighty antlers brought a smile to her face.

The sound of his baritone voice pulled her back to reality. "I tend to agree with the Oracle's familiar, my queen," he said. "It is no secret the bishops are not happy with the union of the two courts, but this is outright insubordination."

The queen sat back down but on the edge of her chair, elbows on her knees, chin resting on her fists. Rowan hopped from his seat and ambled to Aurora. His taupe fur glittered with a tinge of gold, his black triangular nose twitching. The fox was as tall as a fallen Forehelina lilac tree.

As Rowan moved closer to the queen, he was struck by how tired she looked. *The weight of this unification is taking its toll on her*, he thought. "My majestic Muffin," he said in a soothing voice. Aurora glanced at him, her gaze heavy with questions and doubt. "The Court of Dark is due to arrive on the full moon. We can figure this out without the bishops." He pinned his ears back.

She shook her head. "I know the bishops took issue with my choice, but this is extreme," she murmured to the fox.

A knock at the door drew their attention.

"Your Grace, I have a message from Bishop Geddes," a guard called out. Theadova strode to the doorway, his hooves echoing on the crystal floor. The guard delivered the note.

Silence Says Everything

Queen Aurora unraveled the parchment and feverishly skimmed the page, as if the paper held the remedy for the hateful venom her bishops seemed to have coursing through their veins. "Bishop Geddes says he and the other bishops have been delayed in dealing with a dispute between the Selkie Seal Faction and the Oberon Polar Bear Faction. They had hoped to be back in time, but the argument has remained heated. He says they will be back in time for the meeting with the Court of Dark." She slumped into her chair, palm pressed to her heart. Theadova gave Rowan a sideways glance; neither was buying the excuse, but their queen was.

"Umm ... Muffin, that is very convenient, since none of us heard of any confrontation between the two factions," Rowan said carefully.

Theadova chimed in. "Yes, Your Grace. None of my kin have informed me of any problems with the Selkies. The waters are warm now, and the Selkies are living in the coastal waters. Why would they even run into the Oberons?"

Aurora's eyes moved erratically from side to side. "Enough! They would not lie about Fae lives being in danger to avoid a meeting with their queen." She stood, and the wind in the room stirred.

Rowan knew when an argument was over. "Your Grace, how about we figure out what you need for your meeting, shall we?"

Aurora calmed, and Rowan twitched his whiskers at the white stag. There was nothing more either of them could do. They recognized the bishops were not being truthful, but the test would come later if they showed up for the meeting with the Court of Dark.

"Yes, let us continue. We have waited long enough. What do you suggest, Rowan?" Aurora asked, settling back into her chair again, rubbing the smooth lacquered armrest.

The fox took his seat, curling his bushy tail around his paws. "Well, the most obvious is living arrangements. Will King Jarvok move his kin here, or will you build another palace that can accommodate all of you?"

Aurora furrowed her brow. "Leave the Court of Light? I planned every placement of quartz. Desdemona spent so much energy on the design of the causeways to ensure our safety. I—I could not just up and leave this!" She massaged her temples. Theadova shot another look at Rowan. This was so much more complicated than the Fae had surmised.

"Perhaps living arrangements is too intricate to start with. What about the line of succession?" Rowan suggested.

Theadova clucked his tongue against the roof of his mouth as if to say *Really? How is the line of succession less complicated than who's living with whom?*

Aurora sighed. "We do not know if Jarvok and I can successfully procreate, Rowan. Many of the Virtues who remained in the Virtue state have been unable to reproduce, though Virtues who used the last of their Glory to change their being have been successful in creating offspring." Lady Serena was the only exception. When she changed into a Mermaid, those Virtues who changed with her did so without any reproductive abilities, by their own choice. When she met her Oblivion, they all did. There had not been another Mermaid since her and never would be.

Rowan averted his gaze, absorbing what the queen had said. "I understand, but just because you are unsure does not mean it is fact. You must make provisions."

Silence Says Everything

Aurora nodded. "I suppose that, as of now, the rule is if I was to meet my Oblivion, or I was unfit to rule, the bishops would have the power to name my successor. The pool of candidates would come from the heads of the three royal houses, as they already have experience leading. There were four, but I never named a fourth to represent Water; perhaps I should. But I digress. If Jarvok and I were to have our union ceremony before we produced a child, then I guess Jarvok would be the ruler, but if we do not produce a child and something happens to both of us, then I do not know... I see your point."

Theadova took the lead. "What about setting guidelines?"

"Yes," Rowan agreed. "Perhaps if you do not produce an heir, each court would choose a successor, so that the courts stay balanced and united."

Aurora rose. She was not one to sit during stressful conversations. She walked over to a stargazer flower and picked up her water decanter, listening to Rowan and Theadova go back and forth on the line of succession. Aurora glanced out the window and froze. She saw a white cape with a Fire sigil embroidered on it swelling in the breeze, giving her a peek at the deep-red hue underneath. The figure wearing it slipped behind a tree. She put her hands on the windowsill, startled by the sight.

"My queen?" Rowan asked, suspicion leaking into his gaze as he observed Aurora's stance. "What is it?"

Her heart pounded as she clutched at the window, and a breeze swept through the room. Rowan touched Aurora's arm with his paw. When she looked back outside, she could no longer see the cape. "Nothing, nothing. I thought I saw someone or something... but it was nothing at all," she mumbled as the breeze died. "I am sorry. What were we discussing?"

"Guidelines for succession for the two courts," Rowan said patiently. "If you and Jarvok do not have an heir, then you should each pick a successor from your respective court and they should marry. This way it stays balanced. One court does not, well ... excuse the pun: outshine the other." He chuckled at his own turn of phrase.

"Perhaps Desdemona would make a well-suited successor," Theadova suggested.

"We could have Lady Sybella vet the candidates," Rowan added.

Aurora's eyes were still glassy. "I am the queen. I shall decide who my successor is or is not. I do not want to have this discussion any longer! It is my job to protect the Court of Light. I will deem who is worthy, no one else." Her voice was stern.

Rowan's head jerked back as if struck. "Of course, Muffin. No one was insinuating otherwise," he said, narrowing his eyes at her sudden change in demeanor and overly aggressive tone. His ears twitched.

Her eyes shifted quickly to the fox. "Stop calling me Muffin. I am the queen of the Court of Light, not some little one to be coddled or charmed."

"Forgive me, Queen Aurora, I have overstepped my bounds. I do apologize." Rowan bowed his head.

Aurora nodded. "I am done with this conversation."

"And what of King Jarvok? He is due to meet with you in a day to discuss your needs," Rowan said gently as Aurora rose from her chair.

"I am queen. He can tell me what he wants, and I will elect to either disregard or embrace his suggestions.

However, his job is to please me, not the other way around. I am bringing an entire kingdom to the table. He is only bringing... what exactly is he bringing? The Weepers? I have already proven I can go toe to toe with them. Let him come to me with his requests, and I will see what is appealing to me. In the end, I will do what I must to protect us all. I must rest now. I am tired." Her tone was now one that might be mistaken for boredom. She excused herself, both Theadova and Rowan rising as she left the room.

After Aurora was gone, Theadova glanced at Rowan, itching to speak.

"Say what is on your mind, Theadova."

"The queen's attitude is a bit erratic in regard to her betrothed and the preparations," he remarked.

Rowan was mulling over the exchange himself. "She is trying to compartmentalize her heart and her duty. A complicated endeavor."

"Familiar Rowan, do you believe the bishops' reason for their absence?"

Rowan did not waste a second before answering. "No more than I believe a troll lives under a bridge simply because he enjoys the scenery. However, my concern does not lie with their reasoning. Sometimes, silence says everything. I am more distressed over the fact the queen was quick to accept their answer."

Concern flashed in Theadova's dark aubergine eyes, the fox's words striking a chord. "The queen has been a bit on edge lately. I think it is the stress of the unification. The rebels have become more vocal about the two courts blending. I believe it is bothering her more and more. She would normally have Lady Serena to speak with and must be missing her now more than ever."

Silence settled over Rowan. He patted the table in a slow, rhythmic beat, his muzzle twitching, making his whiskers dance from side to side as he contemplated Theadova's words. He had heard stories of Lady Serena as Head of the Oceania House and leader of the Merfolk Faction. She was unique in many ways. Serena and Aurora had been friends as Virtues, and their relationship had blossomed and deepened as Fae. Lady Serena had supported her friend in Aurora's early years as queen. Aurora had seen the Mermaid as her successor, confiding in Serena as one of her most trusted advisors. To lose a friend and source of such love would have been very difficult for any Fae, especially a lonely queen. Rowan exhaled, wondering if he was being too hard on Aurora. Talk of succession would have made her think of Serena, since Aurora originally had wanted her friend and confidant to be the successor. All this would be painful, Rowan knew, and it would explain Aurora's defensive nature and urge to protect her kin.

"Perhaps the Oracles should be present at the meeting of the two courts to offer Aurora and Jarvok extra support," Rowan thought aloud.

Theadova agreed it was a wise suggestion.

Rowan gave the stag a grin. "Let us grab some plum sugar wine. Perhaps Cook has some warm apple doughnut cookies for us."

Chapter Three:
A Call to Action

Aurora returned to her private chambers, rubbing her eyes out of pure exhaustion. The dreams were coming almost every night, but today the queen was certain she had seen him outside while awake. Aurora put her hand to her head. "Maybe I am overtired and imagined it. By all that is light in the universe, I hope so," she murmured to herself.

The monarch relished closing her eyes and not having those dreams. The one from last night was the most vivid to date:

Aurora had found herself stuck in the center of the palace courtyard. Dragor had her cornered while everything burned around her, and she could feel the heat of the fires closing in. Jarvok lay dead at the dragon's feet. More dragons were in the air, circling the red sky. The moon was cracked in half and hung precariously in the distance. Dragor stalked toward her, his black scales reflecting the ruby light, giving him a glow like a smoldering coal. Aurora tried to run, but the bodies of her kin littered the ground.

Every move she made, she stepped on the body part of someone she cared for. She fell backward into a pool of bloody arms and legs. Dragor dropped his serpentine neck so he was at eye level, and his gold-and-purple eyes bored into her, his hot breath burning her skin with each exhalation. The red sky glinted off his iridescent black scales like they were winking at her. The fanned plating protecting the fire bladders on the sides of his neck could not hide the pulsations that let her know he was ready to set her alight. He moved his head quickly, toying with her the way a cat plays with a mouse. He pulled his lips back, if only to let her see his long teeth—stained blue with her kin's blood. He had fed from their bodies. His long black horns were slick, likely soaked with blood as well. But his voice was calm, lacking remorse for the devastation. "He is dead. My friend is dead because of you. You did not protect him. You knew they hated him, yet you did nothing to ensure his safety. Why? He loved you. Why do you not protect the ones who love you? Look around you—the fire raining down is your doing. What will you do to stop this? Will you sacrifice yourself, Queen Aurora?"

Aurora heard the telltale click of the Fire-Breather's back teeth and the sharp inhale just before the breath of fire. She braced herself for the flames, covering her face with her hands. Then she woke up in a cold sweat, the sheets damp.

Yes, that dream had been the worst one yet. Aurora had not returned to bed afterward, instead choosing to get up, and thus, she had been awake since. She lay down now, hoping for a nap before she had to speak with the royal houses regarding the very vocal opposition to the courts' unification.

A Call to Action

Aurora had never found a new house to replace the House of Oceania in the royal house structure, but she needed to do it to balance out the elemental representation. It was another item to tackle today. She would consider the Undines, but with Bishop Caer's affiliation, it could look like favoritism. The Leanan Sidhe, a faction of Fae tied to water, was the next obvious choice. They were matriarchal, led by Lady Puella, who was known for her fairness and her iron fist. The Leanan Sidhe were a large bargaining tool for the Court of Light, as their gift—aside from their elemental talents—was that the Sidhe had a way of inspiring human artists. They were once worshipped as the muses of the Greek and Roman pantheons. When the Court of Light needed cooperation from a human monarchy, having access to the great muses could tip the scales in Queen Aurora's favor. *Perhaps it was time to reward them*, she thought. They would be in the Moon Garden this evening, performing their daily Water meditations. She would pay them a visit.

Queen Aurora drifted off to sleep, her busy mind eventually calming. The world around her blurred as her body sank into the silk bed linens, allowing her muscles to ease, her breathing to slow. For a moment, it seemed she had found the repose she so desperately sought. However, the moment was fleeting. Aurora opened her eyes to find herself facing a very angry Dragor. She was right back in her horrific nightmare.

"I asked you a question, Your Grace. Why do you not protect those who love you?"

She could feel the body parts of her kin under her feet once more, the sickening wetness of their innards sloshing about her ankles. She tried to cover her face, but her hands were stained blue with their blood. She wanted to scream, but she had no voice.

The dragon stared her down. "What are you willing to do for them?" He indicated the bodies strewn all around.

"I—I did not do this," Aurora insisted in a strangled tone.

Dragor was only inches from her face. "Really? Are you sure? You knew Mary was not to be trusted, yet you did not ask the Oracle to read the contract. That put your Fire bishop, Awynn, at risk and led to his demise. You know the bishops do not approve of your union, yet you do nothing. Even now they plot against you, and still you ignore it. Jarvok will die because of your lack of action. Your dead bishop visits you in this realm and asks for your help, but you tell no one. This is your future. Gaze upon it, Aurora, for you did this."

She scanned the landscape—the palace in ruins, the bodies strewn across the grounds, *so many* bodies. Above, hordes of dragons circled in the crimson sky, calling out to one another, in the midst of their own blood lust. "How can I stop it?" she asked Dragor, her voice catching.

"I do not know if you can." He shook his head, his scales reflecting the sickly red light. He turned to leave her, breathing fire at the very tower she and Jarvok had their own knock down battle atop.

"No! Tell me how to stop this!" she screamed at him, but the dragon did not respond. He disappeared amidst the flames. Aurora looked at the chaos and destruction all around her, sobbing. "I will not let this happen. I will do whatever I have to," she screamed to the sky.

"I hear you." The voice was familiar, and Aurora was startled to see Bishop Awynn step out from a pile of quartz rubble. She wanted to run to him, but the bodies held her

A Call to Action

in place. Awynn waved his ash wood and yellow topaz staff. The bodies disappeared, freeing her legs.

She ran to Awynn and hugged him. "Awynn! You're all right!" She breathed a sigh of relief.

"For now, Your Grace, but I do not have much time."

She frowned, not comprehending. "The dragon said I will cause this." Aurora waved her arms to encompass the scene of destruction.

Awynn dropped his eyes.

Aurora backed up, her bloodstained hands going to her mouth. "No," she whispered.

"I am afraid this is a premonition," he said sympathetically.

"How do I stop it?"

He took her hands and held them. "They are plotting against you. You must act. You cannot be passive as you have been. King Jarvok cannot know," Awynn said.

"*Who* is?"

Awynn shook his head. "Aurora, enough with the naivete! The other bishops!" he said, raising his voice. "You are putting your trust in the wrong Fae. They have been against you for a long time. It is why I am stuck here. They are holding me so they can drain my light and use it to overthrow you. They have a plan, though I am still trying to learn it. You must trust me and only me. Listen to me, Aurora. They plan to do something to Jarvok."

Aurora took in what he was saying. "But Pria said you had reached a level of enlightenment when you passed on—the Rainbow Body, I think she called it."

Awynn gave a long exhale. "I did not. That was the bishops capturing my essence."

Aurora clutched at herself, hugging her shoulders. "No, no. I should never have trusted the Dark Fae for that type of information. I am sorry. Was that you I saw today in the courtyard?"

Awynn smiled. "Yes, I am able to manifest for a short time. This is why I want you to request that the Oracles and their familiars are not present at the meeting with Jarvok. They will block my ability to listen in on the bishops. I need to know what they are planning."

"But the Oracles and their Familiars mean me no harm," she said, with more than a touch of confusion.

Awynn shook his head. "You are misunderstanding me, Aurora. With them present, the bishops will be fearful and on their best behavior. The Oracles and their Familiars may sense their duplicity. I need them to feel comfortable enough to show their fangs a bit." Awynn winked.

Aurora smiled. "My dear Awynn, you are a clever one." She embraced him, waking to Ungarra shaking her and calling her name.

"Your Grace!" Ungarra hovered over her with a cloth, dabbing her forehead. "Your Grace!"

Aurora sat up quickly. "What? Where am I?" A wind knocked Ungarra backward.

Aurora looked around, disoriented. She was covered in a cold, clammy sweat. A wave of nausea swept through her. Her mouth watered, and she put the back of her hand to her face. Ungarra made it to her feet in time to help her queen retch into a decorative vase on the floor. Holding back Aurora's long crimson hair, Ungarra placed another cool cloth on the back of her queen's neck, trying to soothe her. When Aurora regained her voice and her stomach had

A Call to Action

settled, she sat on the edge of her bed. The sheets were soaked, as was her gown.

"Why are you here?" Aurora asked, remembering Awynn's words about trust.

"Your Grace, I heard you screaming in your sleep. I came in, and you were sweating," Ungarra said, patting her forehead. "I thought you had a fever."

"Oh, I had a terrible nightmare, it must have brought on a visceral response," Aurora said, satisfied with Ungarra's answer. "Thank you."

"I will change the bed, but first let us get you cleaned up. I will draw you a bath with lavender oils." Ungarra went to draw the bath and Aurora smiled. It did not quite reach her eyes, and she knew it. The dream weighed on her. She looked down at her hands, which flashed blue as if they were stained with blood. Aurora tried to swallow past the lump in her throat and rubbed her hands on her damp gown. She looked at her hands again and they were unblemished—no signs of anything. Exhaling heavily, she stood to take her bath, hoping to wash away the dream, but she knew this was only the beginning: Awynn was correct about the bishops.

King Jarvok received word from Aurora that he was to come to the meeting without his Oracle. Lady Zarya respected the queen's wishes and conveyed she had received a similar message from her counterpart, Lady Sybella. Lady Zarya would accompany him to the Court of Light to meet up with Lady Sybella to discuss how the two Oracles would handle the unifying of the courts as it concerned the Oracles themselves. As of now, both Oracles resided separately, but they wanted to discuss the possibility of living in a neutral location together along with the scrolls, contracts, and prophecy stones of both courts. King Jarvok agreed it was a vital discussion to have; he felt the Oracles themselves should decide the best course of action. He approved her request to accompany him, Lieutenant Zion, Lieutenant Asa, members of the High Council Guard, Dragor, and, of course, Los to the Court of Light for their first logistical meeting.

Jarvok was still figuring out how to unify the two courts. This was occupying most of his time and mind. He decided to take on an easier issue: wardrobe. He stared into his closet, moving identical pairs of pants and tunic tops.

"Black, black, and midnight black Kyanite armor." *I am sure Asa will have something to say about what I am going to wear.* "Ugh," he said aloud. Rubbing his temples. "Los," he bellowed,

Maybe the dragon will have a better suggestion.

Aurora dressed in a gown of sky blue, the color a stark contrast to her crimson hair. The gown was strapless with a corseted bodice, hugging her curves. The gleaming gold embroidery on the boning was in the shape of small, intertwined septagrams. A shoulder piece made of gold leather accented her swanlike neck and traveled asymmetrically across the bodice. A cuff bracelet extended into intricate septagrams that covered the back of her hand. A delicate gold chain linked her fingers, which were housed in gold filigree finger sleeves decorated with bevel-set crystals.

A Call to Action

Each finger had a specific relationship to an element and Chakra, as did the associated crystals: the thumb was connected to the Fire element and was dressed with a red carnelian stone; the index finger had a bright yellow tourmaline crystal for Air; the ring finger was allied to Earth and bore a perfect piece of rose quartz; and a moonstone adorned her pinky finger for Water.

The sky-blue dress was fitted to her waist, and, from her hips, a deeper shade of navy blue cascaded. The billowing train shimmered, while the lighter cyan skirt enveloped her lower body, giving her a true hourglass silhouette. With her hair woven into braids and gathered into a low bun by one of attendants, Aurora placed her crown on her head and went to meet Jarvok in the Great Hall.

Ungarra had a long teak table brought into the Great Hall to accommodate everyone. It was easier for the meeting to take place in the Great Hall with its high ceilings; this way Dragor could remain present, along with little Los. Dragor was the largest of the Draconians, standing fifteen feet on all four legs, the height of a sapling lilac tree of the Forehelina Forest, and Ungarra wanted him to be comfortable.

As Aurora entered the Great Hall, everyone rose. Even Dragor, who was curled in the corner half-asleep, lazily lifted his head. Aurora paused at the sight, her nightmare seeming to come to life. Los stayed next to Dragor but sat at attention, his tongue lolling out of the side of his mouth. King Jarvok took her hand and gave it a gentle kiss in greeting. It took all her will to rip her eyes away from the dragon and look at Jarvok. Once she did, her breathing slowed, and she was firmly in the present. Her nightmare became a distant memory.

"Your Grace, you look lovely," Jarvok said.

"Thank you, King Jarvok." A pink flush warmed her cheeks as he offered his arm to escort her to the table. She accepted, and they took their seats.

The High Council exchanged pleasantries with their soon-to-be queen. However, Aurora noted three empty chairs on her side of the table. The bishops were nowhere to be seen, but before she found the need to make excuses for them, the large doors burst open, slamming back against the wall. Desdemona "helped" the three tardy bishops in.

"Your forgiveness, Queen Aurora, but the bishops were delayed due to complications with the Selkies and Oberon Factions. Or so they claim." Desdemona mumbled the last part under her breath. Bishop Geddes snapped his eyes at her. "I took it upon myself to make sure they made it here without any further delays." Desdemona shoved Caer, the last of the bishops, into the hall, then closed the doors.

Los flew up as the doors closed, startled by the bishops' entry. Dragor used his wing to calm the smaller dragon. It seemed the bishops' energy disturbed Los.

Bishop Geddes stepped forward. "I do apologize for our tardiness, Your Grace." Despite his words, his voice did not hold an ounce of contrition.

The two dragons exchanged glances as their feathers twitched.

Aurora extended her hand toward the empty chairs. Chastising them was not an option, she knew, not with an audience. They took their seats without another word, and Ungarra served everyone sparkling water with fresh Jupiter cherries. The fruit was striated, much like the planet, and only ripened for two weeks in March. It was a sweet-tasting fruit, yet strong like the heavenly body and

A Call to Action

the god it was named after. Ungarra knew Jarvok was once worshiped by the Romans as the god Jupiter; this was an homage to him. All three bishops slid their goblets to the left, the Fae manner of indicating their polite refusal of a drink. Aurora's nostrils flared.

Once again, Los and Dragor swatted their tails at each other, noting the bishops' behavior. The Draconians were observing the behavior of the Light Fae to decide whether they truly wanted to live with them, and so far, it wasn't going well. Remaining in Blood Haven or staying east of the Nempeamp Mountains looked like their best option.

Lieutenant Zion kicked Asa under the table, and she dug the heel of her own boot into his instep. He bit the inside of his cheek to keep from laughing—or yelping. Asa was not going to embarrass her king, and she wanted Zion to pay attention regardless of what the bishops were doing. The blue-haired Fae elbowed Zion, trying to urge him to take the lead and call the meeting to order while King Jarvok and Queen Aurora made cow eyes at each other. As usual, Zion was not getting it.

"My liege, I believe Lieutenant Zion has the paperwork you had drawn up with your suggestions for the unifying of the two courts. Would you like him to read it?" she asked, gently guiding everyone back to the reason they were gathered in the Great Hall.

Jarvok turned to her and swallowed, realizing he was indeed staring at Aurora and stroking her hand. "Oh, yes. Of course. Lieutenant Zion, please proceed."

Zion stood and unrolled the parchment, placing it in front of the queen and king. Aurora felt a shift in the air. She glanced around, becoming increasingly unsettled as Awynn appeared at the back of the hall. She could no longer hear Zion speaking; everything moved like it was stuck in quicksand except Awynn, who glided up behind the whispering bishops. The deceased Fire Drake put his finger to his lips, then moved his long silvery-blond hair behind his ear to listen to their conversation. He pointed to his eyes, reminding her to pay attention to Zion. She nodded and the world focused again, everyone moving in real time once more.

"Therefore, it is important we establish this line of succession," Zion concluded, and Aurora realized she had missed something vital.

"Um, well, I agree we need to, um … establish it. Can I have time to look it over, Jarvok?" She turned to face the Dark Fae king.

"Of course, Your Grace. These are simply suggestions," Jarvok said, his eyes narrowing for a second as though he sensed something was off. But, thinking perhaps he had offended her with his ideas regarding succession, he let it go.

Concentration settled into Zion's sapphire-blue eyes. "Our next order is to speak about the Draconian Faction and the Battle of Secor Valley, Your Grace."

Dragor lifted his head; this was one topic he had a stake in. Los' eyes focused as well. This would decide if the Draconians stayed put or if there was hope for cohabitation with the Light Fae.

"In what way?" Aurora asked.

Zion gathered his thoughts, his hands resting behind his back. The Court of Dark understood this needed to be tackled in a delicate manner. "The dragons have not forgotten what transpired there. They would like some sort of promise their sacred land and ways will be upheld." Zion glanced back at Dragor.

The Draconian leader's neck lowered. Los moved closer to him in solidarity.

"We have already sworn their spawning territory will never be disturbed again," Aurora said, stiffening. "What happened there was a grave mistake. The Court of Light has done its part to make up for it." She knew General Narcissi had misrepresented the facts to get her to agree to ambush the Ice-Breathers. What he had "forgotten" to tell her was that he planned to ambush them while they spawned on sacred ground. If he had not been killed in battle, she would have executed him herself when he returned to the Court of Light. "Since the Battle of Secor Valley, the Court of Light has lost the support of the Grand Master of the Water Kelpies at the River Ness. We now must pay him tribute each autumnal equinox, and our Undines act as guards around River Ness to keep the humans from spotting the Kelpies when they spawn." She rolled her wrist before returning it to her temples. "Ever since that damn Saint Columba incident with the Grand Master Kelpie some thousand years ago, we have to deal with the humans looking for a monster in that lake and have dealt with the responsibility of policing it to keep the humans from figuring out that yes, in fact, there are lake monsters."

Zion smirked. "Forgive me, Your Grace, but those are the Water Kelpies, not the Draconians you have made amends with. They are cousins and not the ones who lost their young. The Draconians did not receive the same promise of protection. If you are to unify the courts, the Draconians will not feel comfortable here in the Court of

Light. As Dragor is King Jarvok's companion, he will go where his king goes. However, this could make for unrest in the Draconian Faction if many feel the Court of Light has not provided sufficient restitution for Secor Valley." Zion glanced between Aurora and Dragor.

Jarvok nodded at his dragon before looking at Aurora with soulful eyes. "I am afraid my second-in-command is correct, and I must side with the Draconians on this, Your Grace."

Dragor raised his neck and stood, stretching his wings. He gracefully walked to Jarvok. Los flew along next to Dragor.

Aurora's nightmare flashed before her eyes. She started sweating again, trying to contain her fear as the serpentine creature stalked toward them. She heard Awynn calling her name and twisted to where the voice was coming from. He was next to her on the opposite side of Jarvok. He gave her a warm smile. She pressed her lips into a thin line and looked back at Jarvok, whose forehead had been adorned with an 'x' drawn in blood. She glanced back at Awynn, but he was not there any longer. The Fire bishop appeared behind Jarvok's chair instead. "Calm down, it isn't real," he said soothingly. He motioned toward the bishops. She nodded slowly as Jarvok spoke to her, but she could not hear him, only Awynn's voice telling her, "It is going to be all right."

Dragor stood in front of Jarvok. The dragon was speaking, but once again, it was muffled. Her eyes tried to follow along as she watched them. Los tilted his head at the queen, his tongue pressed to the side of his cheek like he was thinking. His eyes narrowed.

A Call to Action

Blood dripped from the eyes and nose of the Dark Fae king. As the dragon and king had their exchange, a slice across Jarvok's neck opened right before her eyes, and he began to bleed heavily from the incision. The Dark Fae king seemed unaffected. Los leaned in, staring at Aurora.

Aurora swallowed, trying to remind herself none of this was real.

"You must protect him. They will kill him. They want to kill him." Awynn's voice echoed inside her head.

Jarvok's blood soaked his shirt front, pooling in his lap. Aurora's ears popped, and at last she reached her breaking point. "Enough!" she shouted, and the room went silent. She closed her eyes, and when she opened them, Awynn was gone and Jarvok was unblemished. Los jumped back at Aurora's outburst and bumped into an amethyst candelabra, nearly knocking it over.

"Your Grace? Are you all right?" Jarvok asked. She was sweating again, but this time her sweat had small pinpricks of blue blood. She dabbed at them with a cloth napkin.

Ungarra rushed to her side. "After what happened, I knew this was too much for you."

Jarvok touched Ungarra's shoulder, stopping the house Fae. "What do you mean?"

"She was sick," Ungarra explained just as Aurora leaned over and heaved in front of everyone.

Yagora and Pria both giggled, coughing to cover their immature outburst.

The bishops rolled their eyes.

Jarvok scooped the queen up into his arms without hesitation, and Aurora did not put up a fight. Los flitted around Jarvok. "Call the healer," the king shouted, and

Ungarra did as she was told. "No, Los," he admonished the small dragon. "Stay here."

While Jarvok carried Aurora to her chambers, Ungarra went to find Lady Ambia. Lady Sekhmet, who was passing by, was almost run over by the house Fae.

"Ungarra, what seems to be troubling you?" Sekhmet asked.

"Oh, I am so sorry, Lady Sekhmet, I must find Lady Ambia, the queen... she—" Ungarra was known for her discretion; in her haste, she had said far too much. She pressed her lips together.

"What? What about her? Lady Ambia is helping the Will-o-Wisps. I am a healer. Can I help?" Worry creased her face as Ungarra remained silent. "Ungarra, tell me! You are wasting time."

Ungarra began pulling on her ears, something she only did when she was very worried. Then she grabbed Lady Sekhmet's hand. "Very well. The queen is sick, and she trusts you; therefore, I must as well. Please come with me."

The two Fae run toward Aurora's private chambers, pushing past any Fae who got in their way. Their only focus was getting to the queen in her time of need.

Chapter Four:
A Bigger Issue

The bishops did not feign concern for Aurora. The way Jarvok hovered was making them just as nauseated as she seemed to be. Instead, the three retreated to the south tower, away from all the commotion. The tower provided plenty of solitude amid the greenery in the center atrium, a gift from both the House of Sambucus and Lady Fernia. It was a meditation area that only one group could use at a time. Bishop Geddes felt it was the best place for them to discuss their plans. He led the others in and closed the doors, tapping the quartz light blue to indicate it was in-use.

"Well, that was eventful." Bishop Ward took a seat next to the small waterfall that emptied into a circular stream around the acacia tree.

"Enough!" Geddes said. "We do not have much time. You can cackle like humans later. Now is our time to strike. This works out even better than I planned. She is sick, so if we plant the poison on Jarvok, everyone will think he is poisoning her. Caer, find an herb or flower that is known to display her symptoms: nausea and sweating blood."

Caer's face paled as he repeated the symptoms under his breath. "Bishop Geddes, I think we have a bigger problem."

Ignoring Caer, the senior bishop continued to explain the rest of the plan. "Next, Ward will speak to Ungarra and insist Jarvok stays until the queen is better. He will speak with us regarding the logistics while she is resting. She obviously cannot finish the negotiations. We will be amicable to his demands, agreeing to whatever he—"

"She is with child!" The room fell deathly silent at Caer's interruption.

"What did you say?" Geddes asked in a calm voice, one far too restrained for the information released into the air.

"The queen is with child," Caer repeated softly.

Geddes grabbed him by the coat. "No! Impossible. Why would you say such a thing?"

Caer swallowed. "Her symptoms—the blood sweat in particular. I came across a Fae who was pregnant, and the father was a hybrid from two Fae lines. The child carried three types of Fae in them. It is extremely rare, though, and very few Fae will know the blood sweat is a sign. Most will equate it to root fever. However, I have seen it, and technically the queen would be carrying a hybrid, one never seen before: a Virtue and a Power Angel."

Geddes released Caer's lapel. He fell into a heap at Geddes' feet, moaning. "Do you think Jarvok will know this?" Geddes asked sharply.

Caer, still on the floor, shook his head. "If you did not, I doubt he would."

Geddes stroked his chin. "We must act quickly: plant the poison, kill her, sentencing him to death for the attempted murder of our queen. I was going to let her live for a bit, but if she truly is pregnant with an abomination, we cannot." Geddes glanced at Ward.

"But we will risk his second-in-command rising to power and declaring war on us," Ward said, exchanging a look with Caer.

"Bah, his second-in-command is a troll's ass. He is no match for us. Besides, we have the power to put the next leader on the throne. We will choose a leader who can be controlled. Lord Oromasis may make a suitable king. His ego is his weakness. His many lovers have all commented on his lack of blending skills because he does not know how to treat them. He is always concerned with proving his manhood. All we need do is keep him surrounded by beautiful Fae or humans who turn his head. He will be nothing more than a puppet." A sly curl to his lips, Geddes helped Caer to his feet. "I still want you to find a tincture that will cover her symptoms. No Fae must suspect the real reason for her illness."

Caer glanced down, not wanting to once again be the bearer of bad news. "They were calling on Lady Ambia," he said in a timid voice. "She will undoubtedly know what the symptoms mean."

Geddes pushed him back. "Damn it to Lucifer! Why did you not speak up sooner?"

"Geddes, this might work out in our favor." Ward approached the other bishop warily, his hands raised in a placating gesture.

Geddes stroked his goatee and sucked in his cheeks. "I'm listening."

"Hear me out. No one knows we are aware of this information. If we stay out of sight, we cannot be suspected when something unfortunate happens to the queen and her abomination. We need time to plan and be strategic. We cannot afford to be emotional."

Geddes nodded. "Caer, go and see what you can find out, but be careful. Meet us in the Great Hall—we all need to be seen." He turned to Ward. "We need to act like the queen's dutiful bishops so as not to rouse suspicion."

Jarvok laid Aurora on her bed. She still had pinpricks of blue blood on her brow and had dry-heaved at least four times while in his arms. "Aurora, you will be all right. You must be. Whatever you need, I will do for you." He gently removed her crown and set it aside.

"Thank you. You have been very sweet." She rolled over onto her side and retched. "Please give me a moment. This is most unbecoming of a queen and soon-to-be partner in life." Her voice was hoarse from the heaving and coughing.

"No, absolutely not. I am staying by your side," Jarvok said, indignation seeping into his voice. Before the two could argue, Ungarra knocked on the door.

"Your Grace? I have brought someone to help you." She opened the door and moved aside to reveal Lady Sekhmet. Aurora gave a half-smile to her friend.

"May I enter, Queen Aurora?" Lady Sekhmet asked in an empathetic tone, her brow furrowing as she gazed upon the pale queen.

"Yes, of course. Thank you."

"King Jarvok. It is a pleasure to see you, though I wish it were under better circumstances." Sekhmet bowed her head, and the Dark Fae king nodded, still holding Aurora's

A Bigger Issue

hand. Lady Sekhmet walked over to Queen Aurora's bedside and gave the queen a once-over. "King Jarvok, would you mind stepping out while I examine her? Your energy is very strong, and I am afraid it is shielding her aura a bit. It's making it hard to read her." Sekhmet raised her brows at him. He glanced at Aurora, who inclined her head, signaling it was fine to leave her.

Jarvok lingered for a moment, then kissed her hand. He stood, but not before giving Sekhmet a long, hard glare. Lady Sekhmet squared her shoulders and stared right back at him. "The door is that way, King Jarvok. Or, to save time, you could pull out your member and we could measure it to prove your point, but I assure you I will still not flinch. Now, if you don't mind, I have a queen to attend to." She turned her back on the Dark Fae king and began examining Aurora.

Once they both heard the door close, Sekhmet sighed.

"For a second I thought Lady Serena was in the room speaking through you, because I swear that is something only she would say. I knew there was a reason I liked you," Aurora managed before doubling over, a coughing fit throttling her body.

Lady Sekhmet showed the queen her shaking hand. "Oh, my stars! I have no idea where it came from! It fell out of my mouth. Oh, Your Grace, please forgive me. I heard you ask him for some privacy and when he refused—even though it was coming from a good place, bless his heart—I just got so protective of you."

Aurora squeezed her hand. "It is more than all right, Lady Sekhmet. There is nothing for you to apologize for. But can you tell me what is wrong—why I feel like this?" She put her hand to her spinning head.

"Yes, of course. Let me finish my exam." Sekhmet ran her hand over the center of Aurora's body, feeling for Chakra alignments.

Awynn stood suddenly next to Aurora, startling the queen. "You can trust her," he whispered. "The bishops are trying to kill you and Jarvok, I'm afraid. They want to frame him for your murder. I will tell you more tonight. Now, pay attention. She has news. Remember, do not tell Jarvok, for it will endanger him."

Aurora turned to ask him a question, but he was gone.

Sekhmet had been speaking to her.

"I am sorry, what was that?" Aurora asked.

"I am picking up two auras," Sekhmet said.

"That is impossible. I cannot have two auras," Aurora said flatly. She hoped the astute Fae had not picked up on Awynn's presence.

Sekhmet shook her head. "I never said they were both yours, Queen Aurora, only one of them is. The other belongs to your child."

Chapter Five:
A Fae in the Oven

"I am with child?" Aurora repeated to Sekhmet in disbelief.

"Yes. More three moon cycles along." While Lady Sekhmet explained the symptoms, Awynn reappeared over her shoulder.

"You must not tell Jarvok," he reminded Aurora. "The bishops will use this to speed up their plan and kill all of you. If you could not protect me, how can you feasibly protect yourself, your unborn child, and Jarvok? Be smart, Aurora. Have her swear to keep this a secret until we figure out how to protect the child!"

Sekhmet continued, unaware of Awynn's presence: "The nausea should end in a week or two, but I will send over some milk thistle to help."

Aurora reached for Sekhmet's hands. "Lady Sekhmet, you must not tell anyone of this! Swear to me."

Awynn was next Aurora's beside once more, his hand on her shoulder. "Command her to tell the others you have root fever," he told Aurora.

She thought about it and smiled, understanding his logic. "Tell them I have contracted root fever," she said aloud. "No one must know the real reason I am not feeling well. Swear to me." Aurora's hands crawled up Sekhmet's forearms, grasping for her shoulders.

Lady Sekhmet sat down on the edge of the bed, leaning forward to release the queen's grip on her. She stared into her queen's terrified eyes. "If I tell them you have root fever, Fae who are not connected to the Earth element would be at risk of contracting it and would not be able to see you. King Jarvok would be unable to see you. It is highly contagious." Sekhmet hesitated, catching on. "However, I will be able to. Besides Bishop Geddes, I am unaware of anyone else you would be receiving visits from."

Aurora grimaced. "Bishop Geddes will not see me without his other henchmen. King Jarvok cannot know of the child. Will the Oracles and their familiars be able to see me?" she asked.

Sekhmet brought her fingers to her lips in contemplation. "No, I do not believe so, though their gifts are neutral. They are not connected to the elements."

Aurora nodded in both relief and agreement.

Sekhmet seemed to have another thought cross her mind. "Does this have anything to do with the rumblings about the bishops wanting to stage a coup?"

"What have you heard?"

Sekhmet tried to stand, but Aurora lunged for her and forced her to sit once more. "I never should have said anything, my queen. I am sorry." Sekhmet's eyes welled with tears.

"Tell me," Aurora commanded.

Sekhmet held her temples. "I heard the bishops were unhappy with your plans to unify with King Jarvok. There are rumors they want to take you out of power, though I did not believe such things. I do not participate in idle gossip and thought that was all it was. Anything more is treason! That's all I know, I swear," Sekhmet said, cringing away.

"Yes, I have heard the same. That is why no one can know about the baby." Aurora's voice was flat. "I need time to figure out what my next steps are. Will you help me?"

Without hesitation, Sekhmet gave her answer: "Yes."

A few moments later, the leader of the House of Hathor emerged from the queen's room, a look of concern on her face as King Jarvok and Ungarra rose to meet her.

"How is she?" Jarvok's eyes were glassy.

"She has root fever."

Ungarra put her hand to her mouth. "I have never seen root fever cause vomiting."

"Yes, well, given her stress levels, I am afraid it has triggered her fever to spike higher than I have ever seen it. She must rest. I will return later with a tincture to help. No one must enter her chamber unless I approve them, for both her and their safety. If they do not have a primary Earth connection, they are at risk for the illness. King Jarvok, this means you and all your kin. I am sorry, but I will alert you the minute she is no longer contagious. In the meantime, I will send over a tincture since you have had contact with her."

"If I have already been exposed, I shall take the risk and not leave her in her time of need," the Dark Fae king insisted, his spine stiffening.

Sekhmet gave him a sympathetic smile. "Your exposure was brief. There is a very good chance you were not in any danger in the short time you were with her. Root fever is deadly to Fae who have no elemental connection. Queen Aurora would never forgive herself if something happened to you because of her. Please do not be stubborn—stress is not good for her recovery. Return to Blood Haven. I will send a messenger with details on her progress."

Jarvok tried peering over her shoulder into the room, but Sekhmet closed the door. "I will send Los, my most trusted messenger, every day. He is here now. The small amber dragon—Aurora met him briefly."

Sekhmet nodded. "Fine, send him. I will speak with him."

Jarvok shook his head. "Give him a note. He will have one for Queen Aurora. See that she gets it," he added, more to Ungarra than to Sekhmet. To Sekhmet he added, "You need to concentrate on healing her, not playing messenger." Jarvok narrowed his gaze—he was giving a command.

Already making yourself comfortable commanding the Fae of the Court of Light, Sekhmet thought as she bit the inside of her cheek, trying not to give him a sarcastic retort. "Yes, King Jarvok," she said through gritted teeth. She bowed and turned her attention to Ungarra. "As I stated, Ungarra, I will return once I have made the queen's remedy and packed my things. I plan to oversee her care personally. Please, if it is not too much trouble, can you prepare a room close to hers for me?" Sekhmet now spoke in a melodic tone.

"Yes, Lady Sekhmet. I will ready a room at once." Ungarra bowed at King Jarvok and took her leave.

"King Jarvok, is there something more I can be of assistance with?" Sekhmet asked.

Jarvok was not entirely sure why he was still loitering in the hall. He knew it did not feel right leaving Aurora like this. "No. We did not accomplish much today, for obvious reasons. I am worried about her. The stress of unifying the courts may be too much for her." Jarvok leaned against the wall and removed his helmet, letting his stark white hair fall over his face. He was usually better about guarding his emotions, but today Aurora had felt weightless in his arms. He realized how much he cared about her, nay, *loved* her. Worry overtook him. He held his helmet in his hands, staring at the crown of Kyanite at the top, noticing how the points absorbed the light bouncing off the smoky quartz walls. Since the announcement of their Unity, Jarvok had stopped wearing the full mask of his helmet. Aurora said she liked seeing his eyes. He stared down at the helmet, wishing he had the mask to hide behind right now.

Sekhmet rested her chin in her palm, observing the Dark Fae king. His broad shoulders were hunched as he spun his helmet crown in his hands. She scrutinized the way his hair fell like a curtain of undisturbed snow across his face. He looked small in the moment, she thought, like a little one in need of comfort. Sekhmet sighed, rolling her head back as she looked upward. She closed her eyes for a moment before opening them to meet the Dark Fae king's gaze. "Stay right there. Do not move any closer. I will go speak with her, and perhaps if you stay outside, you can at the very least say goodbye." Lady Sekhmet gave him a smile and knocked on the door. She announced herself as she walked in.

King Jarvok put his helmet back on and eagerly waited outside. Aurora sat up on her elbows, her right hand already on her lower belly. She had only known of the child for a few moments, yet she was taking on the traits of an expectant mother, Sekhmet noted.

"Is something the matter?" Aurora asked, anxiety creeping in.

"No, Your Grace." Sekhmet waited until she was kneeling next to the queen's bed, giving a polite smile to accompany the explanation. "King Jarvok and Ungarra believe you to have root fever. I shall depart to make a milk thistle compound for your nausea. After, I will return to the palace, and it has been arranged I am to stay close to your chambers. I have given Ungarra the parameters for dealing with root fever. However, King Jarvok would like to say goodbye. To deny him may cause bigger issues. I told him if that he stood outside the door, I would open it, and you could, well ... wave or something. Is that all right? He looks like a broken hatchling dragon."

Aurora chewed on her bottom lip. "Of course. I hate that he is in pain. Yes, open the door, and I will say goodbye." She smoothed her hair back away from her clammy face.

Sekhmet waited while the queen fixed her blankets. Then she gestured for her to open the door.

Jarvok pushed himself off the wall, his face lighting up when he saw Aurora through the doorway. "Root fever does not sound like fun," he called.

Aurora shook her head. "No, it is not." She hated lying to him.

"Los will bring you notes every day to keep you company." Jarvok said, trying to sound upbeat. "You remember Los, the little dragon?"

"His tongue is very cute. I like his ear feathers," Aurora said with a half-smile.

"Yes, Los is cute. But please don't tell him that, or he will be impossible to live with."

The two chuckled.

"That is very sweet. I look forward to reading them." Aurora's eyes welled up with unshed tears. *Maybe I could tell him*, she thought. However, just as the thought floated across her mind like leaves on a pond, Awynn appeared next to Jarvok. The bishop shook his head and put his fingers to his lips. It was as if he knew what Aurora had been thinking. Her resolve kicked back in, and she pulled herself together. "I must rest now, Jarvok." Her malaise was rising too.

"Oh, of course, Your Grace. Sleep well." He lowered his eyes.

"Jarvok?" She called his name, a lilt returning to her voice.

"Yes?" He met her eyes with a bit of curiosity. He could feel the change in the air.

Aurora gave a sweet upturn of her lips as she spoke. "All my love and light."

It was his turn to smile. Her farewell was a Fae blessing dating back to their angelic lineage. It was the equivalent of the human saying "I love you." However, it meant so much more to them. To say "All my love and light" was promising your heart and life to another. The two of them had debated the phrase "I love you" before. Jarvok felt humans used the phrase in a flippant manner and too quickly, rendering it trivial and overused, while she thought it romantic.

Jarvok and Aurora had talked for hours one day, debating the term *love* and wondering why humans felt the need to compartmentalize it. Love to the Fae was a non-judgmental energy. It came from a place of purity and freedom. There were no constraints and no limitations on love. If one had to define it or put rules around it, then it was not love. Humans talked about the love of a child versus the love of a husband or wife. But for the Fae, the love of your kin was the same as the love of your child. It was based in loyalty. You would give your light for your child; you were all of one heart, and thus there was no question. Love for your kin followed the same philosophy.

As for your life partner, you loved them, but you did not force them to be faithful to you because of a ceremony, it was because your energies found each other and wanted to stay together. Fae fell in love with the energy of another Fae, not the package it came in. Gender was of no consequence.

Aurora and Jarvok had agreed that when the time was right, they would use the angelic phrase "all my love and light" instead of the plebeian "I love you." Aurora said "all my love and light" to very few Fae: Hogal, Serena, Theadova, and now, Jarvok.

Chapter Six:
Wipe the Smile Off Your Face

Jarvok could not contain his smile as the door closed. He tried to wipe the grin off his face as he strode back to the Great Hall, but the attempt was in vain.

The scene unfolding in the Great Hall did the job for him. The bishops were arguing with Zion and Asa while Ezekiel hovered behind them, ready to back them up. Pria and Yagora had their feet up on the table, feeding each other Jupiter cherries. It seemed they were having a contest to see who could tie the stems into knots the fastest. Pria pulled a knotted stem out of her mouth as Yagora whooped. "Victory, two seconds... ha! Beat that, you troll's ass." Pria grinned. There were at least twenty knotted stems piled beside their goblets.

In the corner with Los, Dragor stretched out his enormous wings. The dragon was getting ready to swat Pria and Yagora all to hell, when he spotted the king approaching. Jarvok shook his head, and Dragor took the hint.

Since Jarvok had come into the hall through Aurora's private hallway, no one else had spotted him. This afforded him the perfect vantage point. Jarvok sat and watched.

"Where is Queen Aurora? What did you do to her?" Geddes bellowed, waving his staff around.

"Us? Our king is the one who offered assistance, I did not see any of you lift a finger to help." Zion retorted. Asa stepped up to help Zion.

Ward and Caer each flanked Geddes. Azrael covered the door.

"Here we go," Jarvok whispered as he saw the bishops each display their staffs.

"If our queen is hurt because of you," he pointed at the Dark Fae, "the unity contract is null and void," Ward spat.

Asa pushed past Zion. "Ward we did nothing, and you know it. False accusations will only anger our king and stress your queen. Go check on her instead of arguing with us."

"Do not tell me what to do, Power," Ward said dismissively.

"I should teach you manners," Asa responded.

"Enough!" Geddes shouted. He pointed at Zion. "You can't possibly expect us to sit back while you and your kind take control of our kingdom."

"Your kind?" Zion asked. "Would you clarify that statement?"

Geddes puffed his chest out. "You know exactly what I mean, Power."

"Oh boy, and now the usual insults will fly." Jarvok rolled his eyes as the arguing took the predictable turn,

Jarvok observed as the shouting match intensified, the bishops complaining about the succession provisions suggested in the unification papers. Insults flew and Zion might have called the bishops some unsavory names.

"You guys are nothing more than troll's pricks," Zion yelled

"Oh yeah, Geddes loved that." Jarvok snickered as he watched Geddes turn red with anger.

Which of course led the bishops to the slight about the Power Angels being "the lowest faction of Angels ever created." Jarvok had heard that particular barb for centuries. Based on the bickering he was witnessing, Asa had stepped up, as he knew she would, defending both his word and Zion's leadership. The bishops pushed her aside, and that was where Jarvok saw Ezekiel get involved.

Most likely not for any reason other than self-preservation. Zeke wasn't certain if he would be joining me at the Court of the Fae or staying at Blood Haven. Should he be staying, Asa would be his mistress; it was his chance to get some brownie points with the possible new leader. Smart Fae, Jarvok thought.

"Good choice," Jarvok mumbled as he watched Ezekiel stand behind his chosen successor to Blood Haven. His eyes focused on Zion, who was taking on Bishop Geddes, the apparent ringleader.

"I will not stand here and have you command me like I am one of your lackeys. Nor will I allow you to insult my king, my kin, or me. Our terms are fair and just. Your queen is taking them under advisement. If you have issues, speak with her, but I suggest an attitude adjustment first. I will take my kin, and we will wait for our king outside before this turns ugly. We have enough respect for our king not to embarrass him during a stressful situation. I would demand an apology, but I do not think any of you are capable of one." Zion turned and gestured to the others to follow him out of the Great Hall.

The Dark Fae pivoted to file out, but Caer made a critical error by putting his hand on Lieutenant Asa's shoulder to hold her back.

Jarvok rolled his eyes. *Of course, the idiot picked the smallest one.* He was not concerned, because this was child's play to Asa. He was more interested in how the others would react to the slight.

Asa eyed the bishop's hand and arched an eyebrow at him. "Take your hand off my shoulder, or I will return it to you detached from your body." The other Dark Fae stopped. Even Pria and Yagora froze, readying themselves for a fight.

"Bishop Geddes was not finished speaking with you," Caer said.

Asa rolled her tongue in her mouth and glanced at Zion, waiting for him to grant her permission to teach the Water bishop some manners.

Jarvok wanted to intervene, but he needed to hang back to see how Zion and Asa handled this. If they were truly going to lead—one at the Court of the Fae and the other at Blood Haven—he had to let them fall or fly.

Zion gave her the subtlest tilt of his chin, and the left side of Asa's lips lifted. Moving like water, she trapped Caer's hand with her right hand and brought her left hand, palm up, under his arm. With an abrupt step forward, she tossed the bishop on his ass. Caer's long, luxurious white cape landed red-side-up over his head. Asa front-flipped, snatched his staff, and with a twist landed behind him. She gripped the pole under his neck and pulled upward with both hands, the pressure obstructing his trachea. The

Wipe the Smile Off Your Face

bishop bucked, panicking, but Asa coolly wrapped her legs around his long torso, pinning his arms and hooked her ankles together, squeezing and leaning back, applying more pressure against his sides. Caer gurgled and spasmed. The other bishops moved in, but the rest of the Dark Fae closed the circle on them. Bishop Ward produced his staff, as did Bishop Geddes.

"If you ever lay a claw on me again, I will hand it back to you in pieces," Asa whispered into Caer's ear. "The only reason I did not this time was out of respect for my king." She released her legs, dropped his staff, and pushed him forward with her heels. Caer fought for air as he fumbled to remove his cape from his head. Geddes shouted for the guards.

Jarvok felt it had gone on long enough. "Dark Fae, we are finished for today. Let us be off," the king commanded, striding out of the hall.

The Dark Fae all stood at attention. Jarvok glanced at Caer, who was still trying to regain his composure, the large red welt across his neck becoming irritated as he rubbed at it. It's as though he thought he could scrub it away. The other two bishops looked chagrined.

"I am afraid to report that your queen has root fever," Jarvok said. "Lady Sekhmet is overseeing her treatment. Since she is an Earth Fae, the disease does not affect her. Lady Sekhmet is currently concocting a tincture to help with the symptoms and speed along the queen's recovery. Instead of arguing with my people, perhaps one of you—" He waved his hands between the bishops, unsure who to address. "—whoever is associated with Earth might want to check on your queen, because I am pretty sure you are still supposed to care." Jarvok could not conceal the derision in his voice.

Bishop Geddes puffed out his chest. "How dare you insinuate we lack compassion for our queen. We were trying to ascertain her status when these heathens attacked us! They are lucky we did not call the Illuminasqua," Geddes said with self-righteous indignation.

Zion lunged at Geddes, but Jarvok put his arm out to stop him. "Geddes, I witnessed the entire exchange," the Dark Fae king replied.

Geddes huffed for a moment. "Of course you will defend your kin."

Jarvok was already shaking his head before the bishop had even finished his statement. "I watched Pria and Yagora play tongue twisters with the Jupiter stems." He shot them both very chastising glances. "I will deal with them later. I also observed you and your henchmen demand information about your queen, even while you knew your kin would never share such delicate news. We have not yet developed that type of confidence. It was nothing more than a display. You launched into an attack on our succession suggestions because that, my dear bishop—" Jarvok circled Bishop Geddes like a Water Kelpie who smelled blood in the water. "—deals directly with your power. It'd be a problem if you had a lowly Power Angel like myself sitting on the throne, wouldn't it? If you were really concerned at all with the good of your kin, you would have made right the events of Secor Valley, because it is a much bigger deal to those very large and very powerful dragons, like the one right over there."

With his fingertips, Jarvok gently turned Bishop Geddes' chin toward Dragor, who rose to his full height.

Wipe the Smile Off Your Face

As the dragon stood, Jarvok tilted Geddes' head up with the dragon. "See, the black Fire-Breather has the respect of thousands of his kin, who are a bit untrusting of the Light Fae since the Battle of Secor Valley. You might want to think about it, Bishop Geddes." Jarvok clapped the bishop on the back, making him stumble forward. Geddes swallowed, still staring at Dragor. "Oh, and one last thing. If you or one of your bishops ever touch my officers again, Dragor will be the least of your worries." Jarvok turned to his kin. "Dark Fae, mount up. We return to Blood Haven."

Dragor took the opportunity to glide a bit too close to Geddes, his eyes lingering on the Fae as he walked by, knowing the heat emanating from his body could be felt by the bishops. Los stuck his tongue out, on purpose.

Chapter Seven:
AND SO IT BEGINS

Dragor sat perched upon the crumbling pillars of quartz in the Court of Light. The red sky cast a suffocating ambience on the ruins. Aurora stared in horror as the large black dragon pointed his wing toward a pearlescent white dragon with a black tail. She recognized the dragon as Raycor, Zion's acid-breathing dragon. The dragon had wings larger than the rest of her body, a common trait for Acid-Breathers. The dragon was shielding something with her gigantic wings, but she listened to Dragor and stooped her head as she retracted them.

Aurora tried to scream, but no sound came out. Jarvok lay with dozens of knives through his heart, and he clutched something close to his chest, gasping for air. When Raycor lifted her wings, a mob of Fae descended upon the dying king, plunging their knives into him yet again. Jarvok swung at them, but he was more concerned with protecting the bundle he was holding. The Fae closed in on the Dark Fae king, their knives clanging until his

And So It Begins

blood colored the ground blue. Then the mob turned on each other.

In the commotion, Jarvok's body was jostled to reveal the infant in his arms. Aurora knew it was their child. She tried to run to them, but the thick mud swallowed her legs, holding fast to her hips. The blood of her kin crept ever closer to her, staining the ground. The more she fought, the farther she sank. A scream edged its way up to her throat, the terror and pain becoming unbearable until it broke the surface. Finally, a wail of agony escaped her lips.

Her anguish drew Dragor to her. His sinuous neck lowered until they were face to face. His hot breath coursed along her skin as if she were standing at the gates of Hell. "As it is above, so it is below. Now it shall be. Once again, your lack of action leads to another's reaction, dear Aurora. Not only is Jarvok dead, but this time he dies with your child in his arms." The dragon shook his head as he circled the mired queen. "Even now, you still think there is a way to keep your child safe. You believe, perhaps, that if you tell Jarvok, the two of you will keep her safe. Bah! You would raise her in a pit of vipers. She would be used against you...both of you. Do you really believe Jarvok would not tell me to burn this place down the first time the rebels took her? Would you put her at risk? How selfish of you. How many mount against your union? And you have done nothing to stop them! Foolish queen. When was the last time you were even outside of your Court of Light? You do not know how to rule. Nor do you know how to protect the Fae you love. This is your future, and notice you are nowhere to be found in these visions. Think about it, Aurora. What are you willing to give up now that you have put this in motion?"

Dragor dissolved like smoke, and Aurora found herself in a meadow, the same wherein she had first dreamt of Awynn. In the distance, she could see him; the underside of his white cape billowed in the breeze, revealing the scarlet hue beneath. The sun was bright and warm. His hair glistened. She strode over to him, happy her legs moved freely again. He sat serenely among the lavender flowers. Awynn glanced up at her, his brow furrowed. Then he stood and went to greet her.

Aurora did not smile as their hands touched. She put her head down and cried. He embraced her. "Is it true? Am I to lose my child?" she whispered.

He tipped her chin up and looked at her sympathetically. "You are destined to lose her, yes. However, you have control regarding the method—if she survives or dies."

Aurora whimpered.

"My queen, this is where you have to make your choice. Protect her or sentence her to certain death. If she stays here, your inaction will kill her, and Jarvok too. The bishops will see to it."

Aurora gritted her teeth. "I will kill them first!" Anger flooded her veins, but Awynn shook his head.

"No, you will not. You are not a cold-blooded murderer," he said, almost mocking her.

"They are planning to kill me. That is treason."

"Fine. Arrest them and have a trial. As per Fae protocol, it will be a trial by their peers, and you will risk the Fae on the jury being sympathizers. They will be found not guilty, and they will still come for you, Jarvok, and the little one. Only next time they will be stealthier, which will increase their chances of success. Furthermore, according to our law, you cannot have a Unity ceremony during a trial."

And So It Begins

As she listened to Awynn, Aurora prepared her retort, but he continued without taking a breath

"However, the biggest hurdle to your plan is, what proof do you have? The burden of proof lies with the accuser. I certainly cannot be called as a witness. If you tell Jarvok the bishops' plan, he will kill them, which will only embolden the rebels." Awynn lifted his eyebrows, hoping the queen would listen to his logic. "You need to send the child away. Let her be raised by humans. Bind her so that she isn't a threat to the throne. Give her a chance at a normal life. Yes, you will lose the babe, but it will be on your terms, Aurora. If and when you best the bishops, you can go back for the little one, but for now the baby must be kept safe."

Aurora ran her hand over her face. "Everyone will know I am with child. I cannot hide this forever. It will become evident that I am carrying." She cupped her hands around her midsection to indicate a growing belly.

Awynn rubbed his chin. "I have heard of a spell called a walk-in. The only one capable of this would be Lady Sekhmet. You would need to find a human infant only a few hours to a day old who is close to death. Moments before the child expires, the soul leaves the body, leaving an empty vessel. Sekhmet must place your child's light into the human's body before it passes on. What is in your cradle will eventually die without its own light, and no one would be the wiser. Once your child's light is in the other body, the physical traits that would have developed will take root, and the infant will appear just as she would if you had borne her. It is a spell that takes great power and skill." As Awynn finished explaining his plan, the sky turned red, and a screech was heard from above.

"My queen, you must go. The bishops are getting closer to finding the right spell combination to steal my essence. Go now and speak with Sekhmet. I will only be able to see you a few more times, for every time I help you, I risk my own light, and you cannot protect me. You were not able to in life—I cannot expect you to in death. Do for your child and Jarvok what you were not able to do for me. Protect them, Aurora."

Awynn's voice echoed as Aurora woke up in a cold sweat. Aurora dressed, her eyes stinging from crying. She knew Awynn was right. She reached for her door to find her daily briefing had been slid underneath, but the note indicated there was something outside her door as well. Since being quarantined, this was the way she was kept up to date on the goings-on in the kingdom. Rowan, the Oracle's Familiar, had written an overview. Last night, there was another protest near the Tora Faction's territory. The rebels had left her a gift this time She opened her door to find a box. She picked it up the pine non-descript cube and brought it inside her room. She slowly opened the box and dropped it. A doll of King Jarvok lay crumpled on the floor with tiny daggers stuck into its heart. Blue ribbons streamed from where the daggers penetrated the doll, to represent his blood. There was a note attached to the box:

> Guilt is an uncomfortable feeling, my queen. Do you have it as you lie with the Dark Fae king? We remember when you asked many of our kin to meet their Oblivion to fight

And So It Begins

> against his forces, yet you now share a bed. Your guilt must itch inside your brain and burn inside your heart. It will grow and fester. We must quench it for you and release you from his grip. Only blood will snuff out the fire of guilt and soothe the itch. Soon, we will destroy the Dark Fae king. Death brings rebirth, and fire purifies all that is corrupt.

Aurora knew this was not the work of the bishops because there was a veiled threat against them as well. She looked up and down the hall and took the box inside her chamber, realizing the dreams were, indeed, premonitions. The doll was almost identical to what she had witnessed in her vision last night. There was no way to protect Jarvok, their baby, and the kingdom without sacrifice and action. No, she did not want to give up her child, but keeping her here was not an option. She needed to speak with Lady Sekhmet and figure out how to both protect Jarvok and send Awynn to a peaceful Oblivion. It was the least she could do for the bishop.

Chapter Eight:
In Search Of

Lady Sekhmet had not been shocked by Aurora's pregnancy; she had sensed it a week prior, but it was not her place to give the queen information until she was asked. What did take her by surprise was Queen Aurora's way of dealing with the news. It was now Sekhmet's job to help the queen in this very delicate and complex matter. The humans worshiped Lady Sekhmet as Mother Nature, Mother Earth, Gaea, and hundreds of fertility goddesses due to her elemental connection to the Earth. She was able to germinate seeds and help plant life grow to epic proportions, either by controlling the conditions of the soil or "speaking" to the plant. She was able to link her own energy with the plant, bolstering its own. This talent was gifted to her as a Virtue Angel. Sekhmet had practiced and honed it until the plant life around her reacted as if she was one of them. Through her years of worship by the humans, her gifts transcended to animal life, humans, and now, her own kin. She could sense fertility and pregnancy and keep the fetus safe until it was full-term. Even now, worshipped by millions, Sekhmet was still learning about the advantages that came with veneration.

As Head of the House of Hathor, Lady Sekhmet was the leader of the Apolline Faction of Fae, but she had consolidated many of the smaller Earth-related factions that needed her resources. As much as Queen Aurora wanted to believe that, in the Veil, all the Fae loved each other, she was out of touch. After the war, many of the factions had shrunk. Now that they were no longer able to protect themselves, their natural predators began circling. Sekhmet had stepped in and absorbed the smaller factions into her house. At the end of the day, the Fae factions were more like their human and animal wards than they wanted to admit. They had natural enemies and innate habits. The Dryads who bonded with the trees did not like salamanders, or any Fire elemental, for that matter. The Tengu Faction protected the peafowl; for obvious reasons they stayed away from the Tora Faction, whose wards were the tigers. The Oberon Faction bonded with the polar bears, and often clashed with the Selkie Faction and the seals. Sekhmet found herself in the middle of heated territory disputes with these two often, their tenuous relationship was legendary amongst the Fae.

There were also the much smaller clans who no longer were large enough to command house status. Sekhmet had absorbed these factions under the Hathor banner and protected them. It was nothing she formally declared, but, rather, a mutual understanding. She did it to be helpful and in case one day she might need friends.

Sekhmet sent for her most loyal and trusted guard, Orion. Each house was expected to have its own set of guards and small army to defend the Court of Light. The

House of Hathor's guards were among the best of all the factions. Orion was their head, a living weapon and Lady Sekhmet's most trusted advisor. Orion was tall. His skin was dark topaz with a gold sheen that shimmered as he moved. His broad shoulders carried his gold armor like it was happy to be there, proud. The armor dripped from his neck to the middle of his chest, leaving his toned abdominal muscles on full display.

Gold was the official color of the House of Hathor, and Orion bathed in it. His intricately designed gauntlets bore the House of Hathor's insignia: a sequoia tree. The gold tunic was accented by bronze lappets, while gladiator sandals completed his ensemble. Orion had one thing the other guards did not: a twin sister named Ora. She was the spitting image of Orion and just as deadly. The twins were born of the Earth. Their parents were Virtue Angels who had used the last of their Glory to bond with the mountains they had sworn to protect, as was their job as Virtues. They became the faction known as the Vilas. The legend of Orion and Ora's birth said the two had fought each other for dominance in the womb and Orion arrived first, while Ora was born with the cord knotted around her wrists, as if her brother had done it. As soon as the two could walk, Ora and Orion went right back to trying to best each other. The two had since developed a mutual respect, but no one would call it love. Orion was considered the better of the two, but Ora was not far behind.

Lady Sekhmet trusted Ora, but this quest she had imparted to Orion only. Time was of the essence. She paced in the main hall of her summer compound, which was built in and around a sequoia tree. This was not as large as her other compounds, but it was her favorite. She enjoyed the view the sequoia provided and loved to look down on the Fae beneath her perch. Lady Sekhmet believed that, as Mother Nature, she should experience each season and all it had to offer. Therefore, she had homes in different parts of the Veil where she felt each season was at its most vibrant. She spent springtime in her compound bordering the Forehelina Forest so she could smell the sweet scent of the lilac trees; though they bloomed all year round, their aroma was at its most fragrant in the spring. The summer was spent in her treetop compound in the Sacred Grove, where the sequoia trees provided shade from the summer heat but allowed for a view of the nearby wildflower meadow. Fall was spent in her cottage compound in the Nang Mai Forest. The orange and yellow leaves were the perfect complement to the fall season. Winter was spent in the Valley of Ignis Grando, or literally translated, the Valley of Fire and Ice. The valley itself was a gigantic glacier, its hot springs heated by a nearby volcano. Sekhmet had found a way to tap into the geothermal heat so she could grow moon fruit and other crops that normally would not flourish in such an inhospitable climate.

Sekhmet walked to the balcony off the main hall. The breeze felt good against her skin. She inhaled deeply, taking in the woodsy aroma—there was a touch of sandalwood to the air, mixed with the clean scent of sunlight. The real reason she liked this compound best was the power vibrating through the forest. Here, the largest living organisms on the planet, the sequoias, surrounded her. She put her hand on the bark and pushed past the rough texture, searching for that pulse of power beyond it, the majesty only the sequoia held.

As Sekhmet connected to her own root chakra, she whispered, "My roots are deep," and heard the tree creak as her hands sank into the bark as if they were melding with it. A red light traveled from her arms, following the veins of her hands and dispersing through the tree. There, deep inside, the spark of magick lay pulsating like a small star, a warm glow emanating from within the tree. The magick followed the tree down to its roots, delving into the earth. Sekhmet breathed in, smelling the rich soil as her magick searched for the source of the power. Past the mighty roots of the sequoia was the basis of what she sought, a white orb of glowing power. If the tree held a small star, the Earth contained a super nova of raw energy that she alone could tap into. Singing in the key of C, she sang " LAM" for I am. Sekhmet energetically pushed her "hands" into the orb of energy and drew the power up. The sequoia acting as a conduit, the tree's leaves bloomed and branches sprouted. Sekhmet pulled her hands away and staggered back, her skin illuminated and her eyes jade green until she blinked, and they returned to their bluebell color. "There. Much better."

The breeze shifted, and Sekhmet knew that Orion had arrived. If he was meeting with anyone else, they would never have known he was there, but this was Lady Sekhmet. With her connection to plant life, it was difficult for anything to happen without her knowledge.

"Merry meet, Orion," she said without turning around.

"My lady," he responded with his usual flat affect. The Vilas were a proud and disciplined Fae. They were known to have no need for romantic entanglements, mating only for reproductive reasons. They dealt in logic and reasoning, with a strong hold over their emotions. They even practiced self-flagellation to keep their minds devoid of sexual thoughts and to punish themselves for emotional outbursts.

"Did you locate what I need?" She turned to him. The sequoia leaves turned to look at Orion as if they had eyes and were being judgmental. The Gerber daisies stood taller in their pots, their leaves crossing across their stems in a critical stance. A dandelion puff released its seeds in anticipation of his answer. All the plant life took on the whims of their mistress. "Yes, my lady."

"Then let us be on our way."

Chapter Nine:
I Knew Him

Lady Sekhmet and Orion's quest took them through the Oaken Door and into the human world. With dusk a distant memory, stars peeked out from the navy-blue expanse above, lighting their way. From what Sekhmet could ascertain, they were in the forest known as Hoia-Baciu in Romania. It was a landscape thick with beech, oak, and wild berry bushes. She inhaled and hugged herself, a contented smile growing as she stood in the depths of nature. *The energy is strong in this place*, she thought, realizing it would make a perfect temple site.

As Orion led her deeper into the forest, she heard the faint sound of chanting. He put his finger to his lips as the glow of torches came into focus. The two Fae crouched behind some boulders to observe. Several humans were gathered, wearing black cloaks—stereotypical demon-worshiping garb. One drew a pentagram in the dirt with a gnarled branch. They dropped a goat's head in the center, and someone called the animal's head "Lucifer."

Sekhmet had to fight to contain her laughter. *Humans and their superstitions*, she thought. *The upside-down pentagram does not represent the Devil, you idiots. Rather, it represented the four elements and the spirit.* Sekhmet herself had taught it to the Greeks to represent Hermes, and before that, in one of her many godly forms had told the humans it represented the balance of the energies of life and death.

The cloaked human drew a circle around the upside-down star and announced, "I have closed the circle."

Sekhmet rolled her eyes at Orion. "They walked counterclockwise, actually opening the circle, rather than closing it," she whispered.

"Now you know why I chose them, my lady. They are not real practitioners," he said.

The human who had created the circle outlined the ring with salt. Seeming satisfied by his handiwork, he removed his hood. In the torchlight, it was apparent he was an older man, with wrinkles creasing his face and a tanned, weathered complexion. His dark hair was tied back and his stubble shaved close. He was a squat man with larger hands and thick fingers, calloused from farm work. He gestured for four others to step into the circle with him. They did as instructed, one of them handing a bundle of fabric to the older man. Everyone remaining outside of the circle stepped closer to the edge, careful not to disturb the salt ring. The head farmer-priest held the bundle of fabric up, and it stirred, a tiny arm reaching from the black velvet blanket. Sekhmet's eyes narrowed. She sensed the child was no more than a few days old.

The priest mumbled, then placed the baby on the ground. He took out a silver blade from within the folds of his cloak and, crouching, made four superficial cuts, one on each of the baby's pudgy limbs. The infant wailed. He stepped back and joined hands with the group inside the circle, who began chanting.

Sekhmet understood a human newborn could bleed out quickly. She could not let this continue much longer.

The ritualists called for the demon Phenex. Phenex was a demon of the Thirty-Seventh Spirit Realm, a demon of science. She listened to their conversation and figured out they were looking for a cure to a plague that had run amok through their village. As a former Virtue Angel, she was well-versed in demonology and knew Phenex often took the form of a demon bird, his attendant an eagle. It was perfect for her needs.

She jostled Orion. "I will perform an illusion on you, not a true shift, so move slowly once I do. Phenex can shift into human form, but I think it will be more fun to stay in Phenex's demon shape. I will drop the illusion when it is time."

Orion gave a slight curl of his lips, almost a smile.

The priest began to sway and wail, as did the rest of them. Sekhmet was unimpressed. This was all an act. He was not summoning anything. There was no power shift in the air. They were doing it because no one wanted to be left out and embarrassed. They were just going along with it.

"Fools," she mumbled.

Meanwhile, Orion searched for what Sekhmet needed to make her appearance—fire, since she was not a Fire elemental. As a mountain Fae, Orion could sense different geological formations. He quickly found flint, striking his sword against the rock to create a spark. Orion chose dry grass and dandelion clock for the tinder, shredding it between his palms.

Sekhmet transformed into a ten-foot-tall bird with thick, oily black wings; gold-colored legs with razor-sharp talons protruding from each toe; a long neck with rings of red plumage; a snapping yellow beak; and red and orange feathers cascading from its head to its back. The most otherworldly attributes were the saucer eyes that seemed to contain every shade of green. They glittered and shone even in the night, but the black crescent irises staring out appeared reptilian. Unnervingly, the bird did not blink.

Orion gave no indication if he was disturbed by his lady's transformation. He merely threw the ball of tinder at the human's magical circle. As it sailed through the air, it became a fireball. Sekhmet closed her eyes and enchanted Orion to have the illusion of Phenex's demon sidekick, a large golden eagle. The fireball landed in the circle, and the humans gasped and screamed, especially when Sekhmet and Orion swooped down among them.

The birdlike creature unraveled her thick ebony wings, the red and orange feathers a torrent of color down her spine. "Who dares summon me, for there will be a fee." As her head bobbed, the plumes appeared to dance like flame. Her voice was childlike and melodic. The bird towered over the tallest human, and the group dropped to their knees, bowing and praying. "I do not like to repeat myself, for if I do, someone will lose."

The priest slowly looked up. "I did," he stammered in his native tongue.

"And who might you be, flea?"

"I am Radu." The man's body trembled now.

"Radu, what is it that you want from me? You are nothing more than an insignificant flea, so that is what your name shall be," Phenex said, her neck swerving.

The man nodded. "I—I mean, we ... *our* village has been struck by an illness of dark magic. We would like to know how to cure it. We offer you a child as a vessel or a sacrifice, oh great Phenex." Radu bowed, his forehead touching the earth.

Phenex glanced at the infant, who was still bleeding slightly. "I do not accept babes as a sacrifice, flea. And you do not please me. You have not paid my fee." The bird raised her inky-hued wings, enveloping the eagle.

The human crowd trembled but said nothing, watching and waiting. When Phenex opened her midnight wings, a tall, dark-skinned warrior dripping in gold stood where the eagle had been. The five cloaked humans inside the circle pushed and trampled each other, trying to run out. None of them even looked back at the swaddled infant they had abandoned. The gold warrior took the baby in his arms, presenting it to Phenex.

The priest was stupid enough to interrupt. "I thought you said the offering was not acceptable," he yelled, emboldened now outside the circle. Orion stalked toward the human, but Phenex lifted a wing to stop him.

In that moment, all of Sekhmet's previous plans changed. With each step the bird took, she transformed. The talons and claws became shapely green legs with scales folding onto themselves. The feathers were tucked behind her back as a womanly figure emerged. The beak melted away to reveal a soft face of such beauty that words could not do it justice. The thick red and orange feathers tumbled into waves of long hair the color of an inferno. When she shook the last of the feathers away, before them stood a statuesque woman covered in iridescent green scales. Her eyes were crystal blue, but her pupils were horizontal slits.

🙰 I Knew Him 🙰

When she blinked, her lids came up from beneath her eyes. She wore no clothes, her distinguishing anatomical attributes covered in scales.

She strode toward the priest, staying inside the circle. "What did you say to me, flea?" Her voice had lost the childlike tone; instead, it was husky and seductive. She tilted her chin, waiting for his response.

The priest swallowed. "You—you said the offering was not what you wanted. I-I command you to leave it," he said, trying to sound confident as he mirrored her stance.

Sekhmet giggled and turned to her warrior. "Did you hear? The flea *commanded* me." Orion growled at him. She stepped closer to the priest, her toes touching the line of salt.

The priest backed up, "Stop, you cannot leave the circle, demon!"

She looked down at the ring of salt and pulled her foot back for a moment.

"The ring binds you, demon!" The priest insisted. He pulled out a crucifix from around his neck and began chanting a Christian prayer, and the entire group followed suit, dropping to their knees and demonstrating the sign of the cross.

Sekhmet winked at Orion. She was going to enjoy this. Still in her demon-woman disguise, Sekhmet stepped onto the salt ring and jolted back, screaming theatrically. "It burns!"

The humans chanted louder, extending their crucifixes toward her.

"Banish the demon back to the bowels of Hell!" some yelled. Others prayed. Sekhmet clutched at her face and pretended to writhe in pain. She waited until she sensed they really believed her act. Then she stopped her twitching and convulsing and stood in one graceful movement as if she was composed of liquid. Sekhmet walked out of the circle, grabbed the first human by the neck, and tossed him into the nearest tree.

Most of the group did not move until the dead man's crumpled body finished convulsing. A guttural scream rang out as the humans tried to scatter, but Orion was there to catch them.

"Put them in the middle of the circle," Sekhmet yelled, finding the priest in the tumult. "You, little flea, are mine." She caught him by the scruff of the neck and dragged him into the circle with the rest. They all pointed their crucifixes at her. She ripped one away and held it to her skin. "What, were you expecting it to burn me? Now you are all true to your faith? Fools! A few minutes ago, you were conjuring a demon. Now you ask God to save your pitiful lives? He is far too busy to waste his Angels on false servants such as yourselves. You were going to sacrifice a child to a demon, and then you abandoned the child in your haste to save your own skin. There aren't too many things I despise, but abandonment is at the top of my list." Disgust coated her words as she paced around them. She picked up the severed goat's head and shook it at them. "And this... it does not represent Lucifer. I knew him before his fall. I saw him after his fall, and this is not him. He would be beyond insulted to know you equate him with a goat. His name means 'Light Bringer'! Do you think God named him that because he resembled a farmyard animal?" She lobbed the animal's head at the group, the carcass landing with a sickening thud.

"As for what went wrong in your summoning spell, you did not use the correct symbol. A pentagram would never have opened the gateway for Phenex. You needed to use his sigil, which you could have easily found in *The Lesser Key of Solomon*, but as usual you humans do not want to work for anything, you expect it handed to you. However, I am feeling generous tonight, so I will grant your request for a cure from the disease that ails your village."

The group mumbled thank-yous for her magnanimous gesture. She smirked, her eyes glinting in the torchlight. "Death is a cure-all," she said, a wicked grin spreading across her lips.

In a flash, Orion slit the throats of all but two of the ritualists, the farmer-priest and a woman. The woman screamed as she looked down at her cloak and hands, soaked in her friends' blood.

"Stay there, my dear, and be quiet. You and I will be having a chat." Sekhmet winked at the woman and focused on the priest. He tried to crawl away, but Sekhmet grabbed him by the legs. "Oh no, you are the ringleader, flea. You are mine." He clutched at the dirt, raking the ground with his fingers. She held him upside down so he could look into her serpentine eyes. "This was all your idea, and if I leave you alive, I know your type. You will take it out on the forest. You are a coward. You will try to burn it all. I will not allow that." With that, she ripped his head from his body. The lone survivor tried to scream but covered her mouth, not wanting to attract any more attention.

Sekhmet stalked over to her. "You, my dear, will go to the village and tell them the forest is protected by the nature spirits. You will say it is cursed because the humans did not respect Mother Nature and tried to use her land as a sacrificial altar. Their souls will be trapped in this forest for eternity. If anyone tries to come for this forest, I will return and trap all your souls. No god or goddess is causing your plague. It is a disease—nothing more, nothing less. Worship Mother Nature, and she will protect you. Do you understand me?" The woman nodded. "That is not good enough. Do you understand me?" Sekhmet's voice grew colder, a quiet anger simmering as her eyes sparked with warning.

"Yes, I understand," the woman said, trembling.

"Good." Sekhmet offered the woman her hand, and she was smart enough to take it, even though it burned. The woman winced but said nothing, and when her hand was released, there was an image of a leaf scarred into the palm. "Go now and do not fail me, or I will find you."

The woman took off running back to her village.

Orion handed Sekhmet the baby. "I already put aloe leaf bandages on the infant to help stop the bleeding. The wounds were superficial. The human did not even know how to wield a knife. However, the child is not healthy. Its light is very dim," Orion said.

Lady Sekhmet shifted back to her Fae form and stared down at the little human. "It does not matter—she will be healed. She is perfect for what I need her for. Well done, Orion. We must return to the Veil immediately and summon the queen. I need to perform the spell tonight if it is to be a success."

Chapter Ten:
A Fae Walked In

Aurora waited at Lady Sekhmet's summer compound, pacing and wringing her hands. She had not been able to relax after she received Sekhmet's message about the status of their plan. Aurora was not prepared for the advancement in the timeline, but if she thought it over much more, she was afraid she would lose her nerve. If all went as intended and Awynn's hunch was correct, she would meet and lose her child tonight in one fell swoop. The thought made her stomach twist.

She glanced around the room to see if Awynn was with her. He had said he was going to spy on the bishops. They were due to meet since she was supposed to sign the Unity Contract shortly. She had conceded to almost all his demands per Awynn's advice, hoping this would draw the bishops out and force their hand; haste begets mistakes. She thought perhaps Awynn would have finished with his reconnaissance mission by now, but still, she was alone.

Aurora and Jarvok had been communicating through the Dark Fae king's messenger, the small, amicable dragon named Los. She was surprised at how much she looked forward to seeing the little fellow. Los was quite the storyteller and made her laugh as he acted out his anecdotes. He also delivered the negotiations each day, along with sweet letters inquiring about her health from Jarvok. The last letter from the Dark Fae king was particularly touching. Aurora carried it with her to glance at in times of weakness, and now was one of those times. She carefully unfolded the parchment, the smooth paper from where she had held it in her dress. The faint aroma of sandalwood enveloped her. It felt like Jarvok was standing right next to her as she read his words:

My Queen,

There is such an appealing ease to your beauty, effortless but profound. I believe that is why it is called natural beauty. You have intrigued me since we first met, and now I cannot imagine a day in which your grace does not act as the light in my eyes and a beacon of hope for what is to be.

All my love and light,
~Jarvok

The door to Lady Sekhmet's private apothecary flew open, and Aurora shoved the paper back in her bodice over her heart. Sekhmet rushed in with a small human infant swaddled in black velvet blankets.

"What happened?" Aurora hurried over to be of assistance.

A Fae Walked In

Sekhmet carefully unfolded the blankets. "She was to be sacrificed by a human demon cult. She is premature—too young to stop the bleeding made by the knife wounds. We need to move fast." Sekhmet's voice was full of urgency as she reached for bottles of herbs. "Lie next to the baby, to the right of her." Sekhmet directed Aurora to the raw cedar wooden table, which was over twelve feet long and six feet wide. Knots in the wood grain ran down the center, marking where Aurora should lie. Large burnt rings in the cardinal directions gave the table character and let her know Sekhmet had been using this piece for a long time in her Magick.

Sekhmet sprinkled fresh moss around the edges as the queen positioned herself.

"What exactly will happen, Sekhmet?" Aurora asked. "I do not want to take this child's life for mine."

Sekhmet did not stop what she was doing, gathering a handful of large, white candles. "That will not happen. Walk-in souls do not steal another's life. The soul grows dim—the original soul has committed to exiting this plane. The vessel will be empty, and we will fill it before another soul continues on with life." Sekhmet lit the candles, forming a circle around the table.

"But why would a soul desire to do so? We do not have souls. My child may not have a soul, even if she is born of the Earth. We are not sure if the Fae born of the Earth are complete like the humans." Aurora could not bear to glance at the infant next to her.

"Some human souls opt out because it feels the challenge of being human is difficult; they may have been lower Angels, and the idea of being confined to the human body is too much. You can understand one might have second thoughts about being away from the Shining Kingdom and his Glory. As for your child, I am betting only on her essence, not a soul. Now be still, my queen." Sekhmet placed two oversized clear quartz crystal points on either side of the two bodies, one at the twelve o'clock position and the other at six o'clock.

The crystal points were the width and breadth of tree stumps and shone in the moonlight. Sekhmet lit white sage in a copper urn and swung it on a chain to clear the energies in the room. She positioned representatives of the elements in each corresponding direction. For North, Sekhmet placed a mound of fresh soil; a bowl of spring water was placed in the West; South was a torch, set ablaze; and a dove's feather occupied the East, the barbs fluttering in the breeze. The quartz points stood outside the cardinal directions, yet still inside the magickal circle. The baby was eerily quiet, and Aurora looked at it but felt nothing. Though she was concerned for the infant, there was no rush of maternal instinct.

Sekhmet glanced at the baby too, and her brow furrowed. "The child's light is almost extinguished. I must work quickly. My queen, place the infant on your chest, face up. You must be in contact with her for this to work." Aurora did as she was told, holding the very still infant on her chest. Sekhmet stood at the north side of the circle, gathering her energy and grounding herself. The energy in the room shifted, and Aurora could feel Lady Sekhmet come into her own power as the room vibrated to life.

Sekhmet spoke in a powerful and majestic voice: *"I, Lady Sekhmet, Head of the House of Hathor, conjure the circle of power by my will and by my word. I conjure my circle of power to contain the energies raised within; as it is above, so it is below. I close this circle; let nothing cross. So mote it be!"*

She walked around the circle in a perfect arc, careful to follow her template until she came back to the northern direction again. *"Powers of the north, powers of Earth: from your fertile ground may I draw growth and stability to bless me and strengthen my power in this circle. Hail and welcome, powers of the north."* As she spoke, the soil sprouted a luscious green seedling.

Sekhmet gave a warm smile. She pressed onward in her chant: *"Powers of the east, powers of Air: come send your winds of knowledge and wisdom to bless me and enlighten me in this circle. Hail and welcome, powers of the east!"* A breeze flowed through the room, calling to Aurora.

Sekhmet continued: *"Powers of the south, powers of Fire: may you bring your spark of courage and inspiration to bless me in this circle. Hail and welcome, powers of the south."* The fire roared to life.

"Powers of the west, powers of Water: may your intuition and sensitivity wash over me to bless me and transform them in our circle. Hail and welcome, powers of the west." The water rippled in the bowl as Sekhmet lowered her arms and walked toward Aurora and the child.

Sekhmet hummed with power. Her normally blue eyes were grey, outlined in bright evergreen. Aurora could feel the sparks of energy coming from her fingertips. The human child gave one last cough and grunt before her tiny body went limp; the two Fae could see her light dim, and then it was gone. They had no time for remorse, for if they did not move quickly, another angel who longed to have a human experience could take up residence in the infant's body while it still functioned for a short time. This was the real source of the Nephilim legend. A human body could remain operating for a few minutes without a soul, but not much longer.

"The vessel is empty. I must take action." Sekhmet gathered her power and placed her hands on Aurora's lower stomach. "I am searching for your baby's energy signature." Her hands glowed pink, and Aurora writhed in pain as Sekhmet solidified the connection to the life force inside of her. "Hold on, Aurora, I have to separate you from her." Sekhmet grunted as sweat beaded on both Fae. Then Sekhmet pulled her hands upward, and liquid light clung to her fingertips, sticking like taffy. Aurora groaned, tears flowing from her eyes, and she passed out from the agony. Sekhmet took a breath; her voice assumed that familiar timbre as she spoke: *"I call to you, the essence of the deep: come to me, hear my plea. Leave your prison, I set you free."*

As the words left her lips, the light on her hands began to unweave; inch by inch it spiraled from her fingers and spun like smoke into the air. The colors of the rainbow whirled in serpentine ribbons above the human infant. Sekhmet watched as the ribbons separated into their color groupings: red, orange, yellow, green, blue, indigo and violet. They undulated in the air, waiting for a command.

Sekhmet spoke again: *"From the dark and the night, bring back the sun. Let your life begin and flow, let your heart beat as one."*

The ribbons reached their pinnacle and descended, plunging into the infant's body at the Chakra points, starting at red for the root Chakra all the way up to violet, the third eye at the forehead. The green Chakra at the heart abruptly opened and burned as the Fire element roared within, causing Sekhmet to lunge back, almost breaking her circle. However, she needed to finish the spell. This unforeseen development would have to wait.

"*By mountain and vale, by land and by sea, I call you forth, so mote it be. You are home, the vessel is yours, the door now closed.*"

The baby's Chakras lit up, and a white light illuminated the crown of her head, bathing the entire room in its glow. Large energy wings appeared in shadow on the wall, seeming to originate from the child. The infant's eyes went from honey brown to evergreen. "My, you are full of surprises, aren't you, little one." Sekhmet shielded her own eyes but followed through with the ending of the spell: "*It has begun. By this hour and by my power, you will grow, and by the cock's first crow, you are one. 'Tis my will and my want. Now make it so.*"

The glow dissipated, and the baby let out a wail, rousing Aurora from her unconscious state. Sekhmet picked up the child. The newborn was pink and lively, her cry a sign of health.

Aurora met the small creature's evergreen eyes; a short time ago the child was of no consequence, but now her heart melted. She immediately reached for the baby. "Please let me hold her for a moment, let me hold my child," Aurora said, feeling a connection and love she had never known.

Sekhmet tugged at her bottom lip. She was afraid of making things harder for Aurora, but she could not deny her this chance to meet and say goodbye to her child. She handed the infant over to Aurora and watched as her queen fell in love.

The only words Aurora could muster was "All my love and light, my little one." Hugging her and kissing her forehead, Aurora tried to memorize her fragrance. She was amazed at how much she loved this little being, and she did not want to let her go, but the idea of someone hurting her child caused a rage to burn. She knew what she had to do.

Chapter Eleven:
One Final Request

Lady Sekhmet let Queen Aurora hold her infant for a few brief precious moments before she swaddled the child in gold silk blankets to take her to her new life.

"Lady Sekhmet..." Queen Aurora choked back tears.

"Yes, Your Grace." Sekhmet tilted her head.

"I have no right to ask for anything else. Yet I do have one final request," Aurora said, the tears pricking at her eyes.

Lady Sekhmet was careful as she answered her queen. She did not want to promise her anything that she could not deliver. "And what would that be, Your Grace?" Sekhmet eyed Aurora, who looked physically and emotionally drained.

"Bind her." Aurora's tone told Sekhmet there was no use arguing with her or trying to convince her otherwise.

"For how long?"

Aurora raised her eyes, and they flashed green. "Permanently. I do not any chance of Fae Magick or elemental connections being discovered. The humans would try her as a witch. Or worse, my enemies would find her and use her against Jarvok. I am not giving her up to put her in danger later in life. She must grow up as a normal human." Aurora spoke in a very logical and calculated manner; in fact, it was the most rational Sekhmet had seen her in weeks.

"As you wish, my queen."

Sekhmet laid the small infant down on the altar and went to a cabinet where the carved gold Hathor insignia glinted on the doors. The aroma of different spices and herbs drifted into the room when she opened it. Aurora recognized sage, jasmine, garlic, and arrowroot. Glass jars were stacked on top of each other filled with dried flowers, leaves, and other items. Jars tinkled and chimed as Sekhmet shuffled them. She pulled two jars from the cabinet and unscrewed the lids, their pungent and distinctive smells filling the room.

Sekhmet took a handful of patchouli leaves and frankincense and tied them together with a strand of black silk ribbon. Then, she reached for a shard of transparent forest-green crystal. The vibrations emanating from it were so strong, Aurora knew it was moldavite.

Moldavite was a rare crystal formed when a meteorite struck a shallow rock in the Earth's crust. The collision between the two caused a gas that rained down in liquid form, solidifying when it cooled. Moldavite was much like the Fae themselves—an amalgamation of the Heavens and Earth coming together under extraordinary circumstances to form something exceedingly rare and beautiful.

Sekhmet placed the piece of green crystal on the infant's forehead, over her third eye. She set another handful of the herbs in the incense burner and lit them, then gestured for Aurora to step back. The baby began to

One Final Request

cry. Something pulled at Aurora, and she reached for the infant but drew back, dropping her head as she wiped at her tears. The cry had changed after the essence spell. It sounded like *her* baby's now, calling to her alone. It took everything Aurora had not to run to her. She had not felt this way before the spell, but now the baby's cry was a knife in her heart.

Lady Sekhmet sensed her queen's pain and offered a look of empathy, but she knew what she had to do. She took the herbs tied with the black ribbon and placed it on a separate gold charger plate next to the baby. Then she lit two white candles on the altar and began the spell: *"By Air, by Earth, by Water, by Fire, you, Little One, are bound as I desire. None shall find your power, for it I bind; no harm shall come to you, for my protection is true. This spell I cast with love and light; no one shall undo it or face my might. Mine is the Magick, mine is the power, now is the time, this hour; by the power of three, so mote it be."*

There was a flash of red light starting at the base of the infant's tailbone with an orange glow just above it. Another flashed at her solar plexus—yellow—and her chest radiated green. One by one her Chakras lit up until a purple orb grew from the middle of her forehead, bathing the entire room in violet. Sekhmet squinted to keep it from blinding her. She took black ribbon and, as she encircled the smooth, slick fabric and tied a knot, the light collapsed into itself and the candles were snuffed out. Sekhmet swayed for a moment on her feet.

The queen rushed to her friend's side in an offer of support. "Are you well, Lady Sekhmet?" Concern was written all over Aurora's face, her eyes pinched in worry.

Sekhmet reached for her hand, breathless. "I am, Your Grace, thank you. You made a wise decision. She would have been very strong."

Aurora glanced down at the now-sleeping child. "May I hold her just once more?" She reached for the infant, but Sekhmet stopped her.

"No, Your Grace. I am so sorry, but it is for the best."

Aurora swallowed and nodded. "I am no better than *Him*, am I not?"

"That is not true, Your Grace." Sekhmet dropped the ribbon and grabbed her queen's quivering hands. "He left us with nothing. You are not abandoning her. You are giving her to a wonderful family and offering her a real chance at life." Sekhmet picked up the black ribbon to make a necklace for the moldavite crystal. She made it long enough for the child to grow into, carefully wrapping it around the baby. "The crystal will protect her, and should anyone discover her, it will act as a warning signal to me," Sekhmet said. Aurora could not look.

"Leave before I change my mind," she said, wrapping her arms around herself. "Thank you, Lady Sekhmet. I will not forget this."

Aurora waited until she heard the door close before she broke down crying. Her legs buckled and she sank to the cool floor, shaking with pain. The emptiness was all-consuming. She no longer had the urge to put her hand over her stomach. The world around her seemed to dim, as if the sun did not shine on her anymore. The colors were muted, and even the wind did not sound the same.

Aurora felt a presence, and when she looked up, Awynn stood in front of her. "Good, Aurora. You saved her. I only wish you could have done the same for me, but there is still time to make up for that," he said. A sodden bloodstain grew over his heart, reminding her of his demise. "Now you have to save Jarvok from himself and those who wish to kill him."

She wiped her eyes. "I know. I know. I am sorry, Awynn." Her whimpering grew louder.

"Shh. No, do not cry. We have too much to do, my queen, far too much. Let us go and plan." He offered her his hand.

"But I need to sleep."

"You can. We can talk in your dreams," Awynn said, and Aurora let out a sob as he led her out of Sekhmet's compound.

Chapter Twelve:
Into the Woods

Lady Sekhmet carried the swaddled infant through the Oaken Door into the human world. From there she traveled to a place that was once the site of one of her largest covens, the Forest of Ardennes. It was here she had been worshiped as the goddess Adruinna. Her following was large enough that Saint Walfroy considered her a threat to Christianity. He attempted to eradicate her cult by installing himself atop a pillar. He vowed he would live only on bread and water, refusing to descend until Adruinna's followers abandoned her. Adruinna appeared to Saint Walfroy one night and tempted him. He crumbled under her charms, but the plan worked against her. The next morning Walfroy lied and told his followers he stayed chaste in his faith. They destroyed all the statues of Adruinna for her attempted seduction of their holy man. Walfroy sought out her coven members and drowned them. Almost all references to Adruinna were obliterated in a matter of days. She became nothing more than a legend known as the Lady of the Forest instead of the fierce goddess who protected the flora and fauna of the Ardennes. She still patrolled the woods to this very day, but not in the Adruinna disguise. Sekhmet had not worn that skin since the sixth century. However, today she would make an exception; for that reason, Orion had insisted on accompanying her.

Orion followed close behind her, ever watchful. He was the best at what he did: protecting and killing, which sometimes went hand in hand. He did not guard her out of servitude. He did it because he believed in Lady Sekhmet. In his eyes, the Light Fae had not lived up to their full potential. They should not have disappeared into the Veil.

The two Fae came upon a clearing in the woods. A picturesque stone cottage sat nestled among acacia, oak, and beech trees. Long willow trees stood next to a narrow brook. Nearby, a human man was chopping firewood. He was tall, with hair the color of sand and eyes like the leaves of an elm tree in summer. A woman picked blackberries and strawberries in a garden sectioned off with twine; she inspected each berry carefully before placing them in a woven basket. The woman was small-framed and delicate, and her hair and eyes were dark like honey tea. She was twenty years old, and the man was twenty-one, based upon their respective lights. Sekhmet had found them only a few days earlier. The events of the past week had unfolded so fast. She had not had much time to seek out a plethora of options.

From listening to their conversations, she had learned that the man's name was Charles and the woman's was Madeline. There was also an elderly woman who was Madeline's grandmother, Marguerite. She was nearing the end of her light; it was growing dimmer with each passing day. Sekhmet was still trying to figure out what it was about the older woman she found so intriguing.

"This is the family I have chosen for the child," she said to Orion. He did not question her; he simply nodded. He trusted Sekhmet and her wisdom. Still, as if on cue, she divulged her thinking to him. "They are secluded, God-fearing people. They have been praying for a child. She has lost two already and is incapable of carrying to term. If I appear as Adruinna, I will not have to be concerned about them telling anyone. They will be too fearful of being accused of witchcraft. If I appear as a saint, they may be more inclined to tell others that God has answered their prayers. She was with child a few weeks ago, so if she stays hidden, she can pass the babe off as her own. The bishops do not have any covens in this area anymore; most of this region is Christian. Aurora's child will be safe here, and the moldavite charm will protect her."

Sekhmet handed the baby to Orion, then shimmered and shifted into her old skin. For her, it was like putting on a familiar gown. She transformed into a towering beauty, long and lithe, with hair the color of amber falling below her waist in loose, untamed waves. Her mane was held back from her attractive face by a crown made of gold antlers. Her eyes were a deep, dark brown like the bark of her beloved sequoia trees, with flecks of gold dancing like fireflies. She wore a long, green gown that glinted in the sunlight as it hugged her supple body. In her left hand, she held her trademark spear, which constantly dripped blood—a reminder that she protected this forest more ferociously than a mother bear guarding her cubs. She gestured for Orion to hand her the baby who she cradled in her right arm. With her long legs it only took a few strides before she was in the front yard of the diminutive cottage.

The humans immediately noticed her presence. She stood well over seven feet tall, and her beauty, statuesque body, and glittering gold antlers meant she was hard to miss. In French, Charles yelled to his wife to get into the house. He held his ax in a defensive grip. A grin of satisfaction crested upon Adruinna's lips. She was happy to see he had a protective streak. "I mean you no harm," the goddess said in her melodic voice.

The man watched her, narrowing his gaze. His grip tightened on the ax, his knuckles whitening. She extended her arms so he could see the baby swaddled in gold silk. His eyes lit up and flicked from the unearthly creature standing before him to the baby.

"May I speak with you and your wife, please?" Adruinna spoke in the humans' native tongue. When the man did not move, she pressed on with her explanation. "This child needs a home." She allowed the heaviness of her gaze to fall upon him. He lifted his eyes from the baby and looked at her, seeming to understand what she was insinuating. He nodded and stepped aside, giving her passage into the garden. Adruinna walked in, and he gestured for her to follow him into the small cottage. Adruinna had to dip her head to fit through the doorway.

His wife backed up, holding the fireplace shovel. She had been confident her husband would handle the situation, but just in case, she had a weapon at the ready.

Charles put his hands on his wife's shoulders, gently guiding the shovel down. In a hushed tone, he explained what was happening, affectionately tucking a stray hair behind her ear. The woman put her hands to her mouth, and tears welled up in her eyes. She grabbed a chair and invited the tall creature to sit, then poured a goblet of water for their visitor.

The man introduced himself as Charles and his wife as Madeline.

"I am known by many names," Sekhmet said to the couple, "but you may call me Adruinna. I have heard your yearning for a child. I am here to grant that wish."

They glanced at each other, hopeful but cautious.

"I require nothing in the way of tribute. I only ask you love and protect this child with every fiber of your being. My terms are simple: tell no one where she came from, and do not mistreat this child. If you break either of these, I shall return. You do not want me to return under those circumstances." Adruinna's eyes flashed a deep green to emphasize her point.

The humans shuddered. "We do not want to seem ungrateful, but why do we deserve such an honor?" Charles asked.

She liked the way he worded his question: full of humility, without the usual human entitlement. "You are worthy of such a gift. I have watched both of you. I know you will love her and raise her to admire and respect nature." She handed the infant to Madeline, and the human took the baby without hesitation.

Madeline cried tears of joy. "Thank you, thank you. She is perfect." The goddess could see that the woman was already in love with the child.

"One more item," Sekhmet said. "The necklace on the child must stay there. It is a protection amulet. If anyone ever comes looking for her or asks too many questions about her, light a fire and burn jasmine. This will signal me to come. If the necklace is removed from her for a time I deem too long and the fire is not burned, I will come. I will bring death first and ask questions after. Are we clear?"

Both humans swallowed hard and nodded.

A shuffling sound interrupted their talk, and an old woman with hair in a long braid as white as a cloud on a summer's day entered from a back room. "Do I hear a visitor?" she asked in a strained voice. Her face was weathered, and she had one grey-blue eye; the other was similar in color but covered in a milky cataract. The old woman felt around for the chair Madeline had moved for the goddess. The woman was blind and searching for her familiar markers.

"Grandmother. We have a guest," Madeline said. She reluctantly handed the child to her husband and helped the old woman to a seat.

"And a baby, I hear," the woman said.

Madeline looked at her grandmother quizzically. "How did you know? She did not even cry."

The older woman gave a sly smile. Her age lines vanished for a brief second, revealing a glimpse of the glowing beauty that lay behind the mask of time. "I could hear the child breathing. Infants breathe faster and most uneven at such a young age. And with whom do I have the pleasure of meeting?" The elderly woman motioned in the direction of the goddess.

"Grandmother, this is our friend Adruinna." Madeline turned to smile at the goddess. "Adruinna, this is my grandmother Marguerite."

"It is a pleasure," the goddess said.

Marguerite sucked in a sharp breath and coughed. "Madeline, dear, would you get me some water?"

The baby started crying. The two young humans were getting a quick taste of being new parents. "Go take care of the baby, both of you," Marguerite said after her granddaughter handed her the cup of water. The husband and wife did not need to be told twice. They practically jumped out of the room to care for their child.

"So, you have returned, goddess, after all this time, and you brought a Faerie child with you," Marguerite said to Adruinna. The goddess raised her eyebrows and parted her lips to speak, but the old woman waved her hand. "Do not try to deny it." The woman pointed to her cloudy eye. "I am a descendant of seers, from your very own coven. I can see what most humans cannot. I see your form, Lady of the Forest, and yes, I know of the Faeries." The old woman leaned forward as if she could really see. Sekhmet smiled. The human knew things, but not everything. "Did you give the child to them because of me?"

Lady Sekhmet shook her head out of reflex. "No, I chose them because I knew they would love the child. The baby's gifts are bound, and she is under my protection."

The old woman pursed her lips. "Whose child is she?"

The goddess laughed. "I cannot tell you, old woman. I would have to end you if I did." She figured her answer would stop this questioning.

"Perhaps that is why I am asking," the old woman said. The goddess' head jerked back. "My gifts in my old age have become stronger but less controllable, and eventually I will figure it out. If you truly want to protect her and my family, it is best to kill me. I ask you for a merciful death. I will see through the spell and possibly weaken it. Use me to keep them quiet. I love them, but they will see the child as a blessing from their God. Regardless of what they say or how many times you ask them to promise you, they will not keep your secret. You must scare them into obedience. They do not understand the old ways. Kill me and leave them a message with my blood."

Sekhmet was impressed with the older human, which was very rare, but she took some credit since the woman had descended from her coven. "You make a compelling argument. I promise a swift death. She is the child of the queen of the Seelie Court." Sekhmet used the human terms for their kind. "The queen has mortal enemies who will use the child against her."

"And the father?" Marguerite inquired.

"Not available to provide the child with protection. He has his own set of enemies." *It was a partial truth,* Sekhmet thought. She felt a tinge of guilt at disposing of a human with such an agile mind.

Charles and Madeline came back into the room. "We did not ask if she has a name," Madeline said.

Marguerite spoke up. "I always loved the name Angélique. It means 'like an Angel.' Don't you agree, Adruinna?"

The goddess smiled at the old woman with a new appreciation. *Perhaps this human is too smart for her own good,* she thought, *in which case killing her is not such a bad idea after all. My guilt is assuaged.*

"I adore it, Grandmother! Angélique, it is perfect." Madeline cooed at the infant.

Adruinna. "I must take my leave. Remember what we discussed. Be well."

Madeline handed Angélique to her husband and ran over to the goddess. She hugged her and kissed her hand.

"Thank you. I am indebted to you. You have healed my heart. I am forever grateful," Madeline managed between sobs.

Adruinna smiled and caressed the human's face with the back of her hand. "You are most welcome, my dear." She glanced at the old woman and dipped her head as she left.

Sekhmet waited until she was out of sight before shaking off her disguise like a snake shedding her skin.

"Did it go well, my lady?" Orion asked.

"It went well, but you will be making an appearance here tonight. The old woman who resides with them needs to be disposed of."

"She is a threat?"

"No, not directly. She is a descendant of the seers from my old coven and has the gift of sight. I believe she knows more than she is letting on. I have promised her a swift death in exchange for her silence. We shall use her to ensure they stay quiet," Sekhmet said calmly. "I will draw up a message for you to leave in her blood."

Orion nodded. "A throat slashing will work best if I am to transcribe a message in blood."

"I agree. It will avail her a quick death. Come, I must prepare for this new wrinkle in our plan and speak to the queen."

Chapter Thirteen:
Partners in Crime

Sekhmet sat across from her queen, the silence heavy between them. Aurora had given the other Fae permission to send her only child away to be raised by humans to save the life of the infant. Tomorrow, Aurora would make yet another sacrifice in the name of love. For thousands of years, Aurora had placed her kin's needs above her own, and as far as Sekhmet knew, her queen never made a fuss. Those acts of self-sacrifice were nothing in comparison to what she had done today, and yet she still had not so much as grumbled about the responsibility of being a queen.

Sekhmet did not feel right about leaving Aurora alone to complete the last few details of the plan. She was confident Orion could handle his job—her queen needed her.

Aurora lifted her head as she signed her name to the final copy of the two letters. She held them up, scrutinizing them to make sure they were identical in every way. The letters contained her confession, including the why and how as well as where to find their child when Jarvok was ready. It had been Sekhmet's idea to construct two letters. Knowing Jarvok's temper and pride, there was a very good chance he would destroy the first letter when Aurora's plan unfolded tomorrow. A second letter was a logical idea should the first become collateral damage; it would be delivered to him once he calmed down, ensuring he would be more receptive to its contents. The two Fae agreed Sekhmet would hold the letters for safekeeping. Aurora handed her both letters with her royal seal attached for authenticity.

Sekhmet tucked the letters into her cloak. She was aware of what was to be done. They reviewed what would happen after Jarvok arrived to sign the Unity Contract. Awynn had said the bishops planned to strike on this day, and though Aurora explained to Sekhmet the scope of the bishop's scheme, she did not mention the source of her information. Geddes apparently planned to use the Galena blade as a decoy. Since Galena had a slight iron composition, it could cut Fae but not kill them. Geddes was going to replace the Galena blade with a fake. However, his would have a special accessory: a hollow tip filled with liquid iron so that, as Aurora cut her finger to sign the contract in blood, she would inject herself with pure liquid iron. She would be dead within minutes.

The discovery of the Fae's vulnerability to iron was made by Hogal the metal Gnome, before the war. His connection was to Earth, with a special affinity for minerals. While mining, he had found a dark, almost black, ore, but when he had attempted to touch it, it burned his hands, his stomach twisted, and his skin itched. Other Fae reported similar symptoms around deposits of this ore. Some Fae had comparable reactions when they encountered human-created objects containing iron. Weaker Fae or little ones even had fatal reactions to it. Many Spelaions met their Oblivion removing iron ore deposits from areas where whole factions had become sick from the metal. None of the Fae could figure out why it had this effect on them, though iron did seem to repel most elemental Magick. Even stronger Earth elementals, who were able to stave off the effects for an extended period of time, eventually succumbed to its prowess, so no Fae had been willing to figure it out.

If the bishops injected enough of the liquid directly into Aurora's bloodstream, she would die. As if dying from iron poisoning wasn't painful enough, Aurora was positive the bishops had added some other nasty concoction to the iron solution to make sure she would die an agonizing death. Her demise would prevent the contract from being signed, and a message would come in from an anonymous source to check King Jarvok's suite, where the real Galena blade would be found. Given that it took extreme temperatures to melt iron, some would conclude that his Fire-Breather must have been the one to melt it. It would not be a huge leap for many since there was such mistrust among their kin for the Dark Fae. King Jarvok would be taken into custody, along with his lieutenants as accessories. As far as the bishops were concerned, all of their threats would be eliminated in one fell swoop.

The bishops' plan was crude, but it had merit. Aurora decided to turn the tables on them. The plan she and Awynn had devised was cunning but called for her to make the ultimate sacrifice: her child, her love, and her kingdom. She hoped it would not mean her light, but there was a chance that would be lost too.

Aurora's dress was the perfect metaphor for what was going on in her head. The top half of her dress was a dark navy blue with a demure neckline and long sleeves. It was elegant, but a misdirection, because the cream-colored skirt had a thigh-high slit and a flurry of multicolored sparrows flying across the fabric. It was a complete detour from her unusual regal attire. It was a practice in the art of distraction that said: *sure, I'm simple and elegant up top, but I am controlled chaos underneath it all. Yes, I have something up my sleeve, but you will never know until it is too late.* Even her aura had changed: she gave off the energy that she was not playing anymore. She had a child and lover to save and a kingdom to protect.

Sekhmet, for her part, wore a floor-length traditional white gown with long split sleeves and an empire waist. The watercolor print boasted red dahlias scattered across the bodice.

Sekhmet knew there was no point in asking Aurora if she was having second thoughts or if she was ready for tomorrow. How did one prepare to upend their life, to betray the only love they had ever known, and to give up their kingdom? The answer was that one could not. So why even ask? Sekhmet took a different approach: distraction. The rising sun was inevitable, and there was no use pretending they could stop it. Instead, she tried to make the moments that passed a little less painful.

Aurora had showed Sekhmet she trusted her. While Sekhmet could never repay her for the demonstration of confidence, she could let the queen in on a few insights of her own, the same way Lady Serena had done when she was alive. Sekhmet had heard stories about how the two of them would share their philosophies on life, and how that had shaped the ethics of the Court of Light. Most of all, these conversations had helped Aurora keep her sanity. Sekhmet decided to step in and fill the void left by Serena, if only for a few hours. Aurora was sharing so much, it only felt right to share something of herself.

"Since we are here together in the solitude of your chambers, I feel now is the best time to make a confession to you, Your Grace," Sekhmet said, casting her eyes down so only her long pastel lashes could be seen.

Aurora stopped smoothing out her skirt and arched her right eyebrow at her newly minted partner in crime. "A confession, Lady Sekhmet? After all we have done and have yet to do? What could you possibly have to confess?"

Sekhmet fussed with one long sleeve. "I went to see... Well, I had heard all the stories about the wine and the turning one fish into thousands... so I had to see for myself. I went to see ... Him."

Chapter Fourteen:
The Jesus Factor

"*Him?*" Aurora asked. In truth she had no need of clarification. She did indeed know exactly the human to which Lady Sekhmet referred, but the mixture of shock and curiosity caused her to question Sekhmet's meaning.

Sekhmet exhaled, unable to meet her queen's eyes. "Yes ... Him." She did not wait for Aurora to ask the inevitable follow-up question. "During his execution." She straightened her shoulders, preparing for admonishment from her queen.

Aurora had never forbidden anyone from contacting Him. However, after the parting of the Red Sea and the run-in with the prophet Moses, it was greatly discouraged for the Fae to interact with any religious prophets in case they felt compelled to reveal their angelic nature. If they were truly Fae, they needed to leave the past in the past.

However, Aurora merely crinkled her nose upon hearing Sekhmet's answer. "You went during his execution? Morbid curiosity?"

Sekhmet shrugged, her rainbow-streaked hair tumbling forward, causing a few pieces to loosen from her braids and obscure her eyes.

Aurora leaned forward and gently pushed the strands from her friend's face. She knew Sekhmet was trying to hide from the world. "Well, what happened?" Aurora asked.

Sekhmet shook her head, not sure now if she wanted to divulge the tale.

Aurora sat back, giving her some room to breathe. However, when Sekhmet did not answer, Aurora broke the silence. "I have a bit of a confession to make too." Sekhmet did not look up, but she did stop fiddling with her long braid. "After the incident with Moses and the Red Sea, I kept tabs on them. I followed the Israelites into the desert. For weeks I checked in, watching them. It was so very long ago; I cannot remember exactly how much time passed. However, I do recall that they were hot and thirsty. I thought, at any moment, they would be praying to a rain goddess for a reprieve. But instead, I was overtaken by power; while my head told me to fight, my body told me to surrender, and my heart told me something different entirely. My heart said one word: *home*.

"I was there when our Creator spoke to the humans for the first time. I heard his voice, and Sekhmet, I cried. I wanted to run to Him, throw my arms around Him, and tell Him to take me back, but I did not. Before I could move, He was gone." Aurora turned her head away from Sekhmet, not wanting to show the longing in her eyes. Sekhmet was silent. Aurora wanted to break the awkwardness, so she kept talking. "I do not know why I followed them. There was something about the human Moses—his light was strange. I think I saw it as a link to the past. He reminded me of the Creator, but I did not know how that was possible." Aurora's brow furrowed. Now that she was saying it aloud, the story seemed so trite.

But Sekhmet nodded as though she understood. "You heard Father's voice?" Her tone was hushed, almost reverent.

Aurora hesitated. She had not referred to Him as Father since she renounced Him that day on the mountaintop when her last feather fell. "I heard our Creator speak to them, and it was a beautiful agony. To hear Him speak after we had prayed and sung for so long. I think—this is hard for me to say, Sekhmet—I think that I threw myself into the war with the Dark Fae because I blamed them for our abandonment. I wanted to bring stability to our kin. I wanted us to be safe, and I think I convinced myself the Dark Fae were siding with our Creator and that justified my anger." It was Aurora's turn to look for admonishment.

Sekhmet put her hand on her queen's leg, giving her a gentle squeeze. "I understand completely."

Aurora lifted her tear-stained face. "You must believe me. I never put our kin in danger unnecessarily." Aurora's voice hitched.

"Why would you even feel the need to say that to me? Of course you didn't. You didn't declare the war! You led us through a brutal time, Queen Aurora. No one blames you." Sekhmet clutched her queen's hand. "I think we all wanted a piece of home. It is why you followed Moses, and it is why I sought Him out." Sekhmet loosened her grip on Aurora's hand, already lost in her own recollections.

"When did you see Him?" Aurora asked gently.

Sekhmet closed her eyes for a moment as if she was ripping herself away from a memory. "It was April 3, 33

AD by the human calendar, thirty days before Beltane for us. It was a warm spring day. We had just lost the last of the Abada Faction. I remember Lady Lolita dying in my arms while Pria wore her horn as a trophy around her neck. I couldn't stand against Pria; I wanted to avenge Lolita, but it would have been futile. I walked away to mourn and found myself wandering among the humans. They were all talking about the son of God, and maybe it was my grief, I do not know, but I followed the crowd to the Hill of Skulls to witness someone else's pain." Sekhmet's voice was hazy, adrift in her memory. "He was slight in build. Dark, sun-kissed complexion with auburn hair, matted with crimson streaks of blood. His left eye was swollen shut. Purple and blue welts marred His face. They drove metal nails into His wrists and one through both ankles as He screamed in agony. For the final piece of torment, I witnessed them place Him upon a wooden contraption in the shape of an *X* and let him hang there." Her eyes were glassy as she recounted the scene she had witnessed so long ago.

Aurora said nothing, too engrossed and horrified by Sekhmet's tale.

"Then I heard Him pray, and His voice resonated with me. It was like a bell being rung that had been dormant for years. The sound in my heart was clear and bright as I listened to Him. His voice sang to me while he called to the heavens." Sekhmet took a sharp breath, and then gathered herself, shaken by the recollection. "I can say for certain, my queen, His light was as close to the Shining Kingdom as I have seen in a thousand years. Even as dim as it was, the power that hummed from Him was not like a human who had been graced by an Angel. I wanted to get closer, to rescue Him from the wolves encircling him, but I am ashamed to say that I didn't. I just gave Him one last look before His light was extinguished. I was afraid of what I would do if I stayed. I tried to forget what I had seen and felt. However, my mind and heart yearned for that light again and again." Sekhmet blinked back tears as she locked eyes with Aurora.

The queen was not sure what she wanted the outcome to be—was He truly the Son of the Creator or just another human tall tale? *Perhaps a little of both.* "He really is like the humans say?" she whispered, her heart pounding.

Sekhmet shook her head. "Please let me finish, my queen, before we draw conclusions of that magnitude. Once you hear of my journey, you will see that flippant observations are purely human."

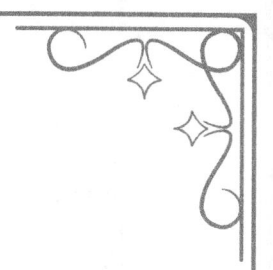

Chapter Fifteen:
The Mountain Comes to the Fae

Aurora scooted forward on the bed, barely noticing. Her fingers twisted in the coverlet, and she hung on to every word Sekhmet uttered.

"After witnessing the man known as Jesus," Sekhmet said, "I sought out as much information as I could about him. I read the Jewish Torah and found misinterpretations of Fae events represented as acts of Faith and the Creator's influence. We both know who parted the Red Sea and what caused the plagues of Egypt—Fae, not Him. The whale swallowing Jonah was nothing more than the Selkies' guardians getting overprotective when the humans sailed too close to their territory. It seems the humans mistook many Fae events, giving the Creator credit for our assistance. I wondered if it was a mistake or a plan, some kind of divine intervention."

Sekhmet had continued with her education over the years, reading up on the humans' religion and trying to discern why some considered Jesus to be important while others did not. She had tried to find his disciples, but most of them were killed right after his death, leaving her unable to get a clearer picture of his teachings and how the Fae were involved. In fact, it was not until the fourth century that she could find written evidence with details of Jesus' death. However, the human description was all wrong. "I realized in that moment that these were not eyewitness accounts, but fables told by the fire—passed down from one to another, colored by time and history. Still, as humans transcribed and told stories about Jesus, it seemed the world changed. I decided I needed to find a prophet and see it unfold for myself."

Sekhmet pointed to her chest. "I was in the eastern area of our territory following the spread of Christianity into our pagan tribes. Mecca was an important site for us, and Christian groups were overtaking our temples. My priestesses called out for help to hold back an aggressive invasion. I arrived to hear stories of a group of believers being led by a man who was visited by the Archangel Gabriel, and he was deemed a great prophet. This same prophet, who the people called Muhammad, was destroying the pagan temples and statutes in Kaaba. He was touting a new religion after Gabriel's visit, said Gabriel commanded him to read the Quran."

Aurora put her finger to her chin, recalling having to deal with fighting between tribes of Fae worshippers and a new prophet. "Yes, our ways were coming under fire at the time," she said.

"Muhammad was a passionate speaker." Sekhmet gazed away for a moment, rubbing the side of her cheek. "His light was identical to Jesus' light."

"What?" Aurora leaned forward, her eyes wide, and hit the bed. "Tell me."

Sekhmet slumped and dropped her arms to her side, as if she had been carrying a heavy boulder and was about to finally release it. "Muhammad's light was just as bright and awe-inspiring, and if I had ever seen Moses', I believe his would have been as well."

Aurora stood and paced. "That is impossible, Sekhmet. I do not understand. This... is..." She turned to her friend, rubbing her temples. Aurora wanted to tell Sekhmet she was wrong, but something about what the Fae had said was ringing true, although the queen was not sure what.

"My queen, listen to me. It is possible they shared the same light."

"How?" Aurora slapped her hands on the tops of her thighs.

"Because they were all the same being," Sekhmet said, meeting her queen's gaze.

Everything suddenly crystallized. It was as though Aurora had been walking around in a fog for centuries, and it had finally lifted, revealing the landscape. Her legs went weak, and she crumpled onto the bed. "How?"

Sekhmet took a long inhale, knowing what she was about to explain would rock Aurora to her very core. "I believe our Creator was all three of these prophets. I do not think Jesus was the son of God. He *was* God. I have surmised He walked among the humans as Moses. He saw how He was more feared than loved by them, and so He created the illusion of the son of God because it sounded less intimidating. I am convinced He is angry at us for being worshiped and He wanted to strengthen His power base by creating different monotheistic religions. He is trying to teach us a lesson. In the sacred books of these religions He says that they are not to worship false idols and that He is their one true God. That is in direct retaliation to our ways." Sekhmet tapped her index finger to her lips, eyes darting side to side. "He bestowed different religions as an *illusion* of choice. What the Creator did not count on was the infighting—the way humans use religion to justify certain behaviors. I have yet to figure out how Lucifer plays into this chess game." She shrugged, indicating Lucifer's involvement was a mystery for another day.

Sekhmet turned her bluebell eyes back toward her queen and smoothed her skirt as if to wipe away her thoughts. "I believe He is all of the gods in the monotheistic religions. He is the central figure who walked the Earth; the light I saw in both Jesus and Muhammad were the same power as that in the Shining Kingdom. He manifested himself as the prophet of each religion to walk in this world. The humans have added their own color to the events as time has passed, giving them mythic proportions. I think the Creator enjoys the mystery. It is all to push his agenda and secure his power, as it teaches his angelic children a lesson. The humans are a means to an end, my dear queen. We actually take priority in His mind."

Chapter Sixteen:
Is That All There Is?

Orion arrived at the cottage well past what the humans referred to as the witching hour. It was the dead of night, when no prayers were taking place, and no human had any reason to be out of bed. However, as he walked up to the small stone cottage, he noticed a figure waiting on a stool, a hooked walking cane beside her. She beckoned for Orion to come closer.

The Vila Fae crooked his head, finding this a most intriguing development. He did not hurry for the human; regardless of how interesting they might seem, no one was worthy of him rushing.

The old woman matched the description Lady Sekhmet had given him. "Marguerite." Orion's deep baritone voice resonated in the night air.

The woman nodded. "My undoing, I presume." She stood, using the cane to get to her feet. "I thank you for not bothering with a disguise. It makes this a much more honest exchange."

"How did you know?"

The old woman pointed toward her milky eye. "Not everything is seen with our eyes."

"You are welcome." Orion readied his blade, but Marguerite held her hand up.

"Before we do this, do you have the message for my family? I did not agree if it was to be done in vain." Her voice was stern, almost chiding him.

Orion quirked his eyebrow at the woman. "I do."

The old woman mocked his eyebrow arch, and Orion jerked his head back.

She pointed her cane at him. "I would like to hear it. I am giving my blood for it after all."

The Fae exhaled, but since she would be dead in a minute, it was inconsequential if she heard it. "Very well." He unrolled the parchment Lady Sekhmet had given him, and read it to the woman:

Charles and Madeline,

I gave you a most wondrous gift, with the terms to love her and tell no one of her true origin. It has not been but a day, and yet your grandmother has betrayed this covenant. She saw this gift as a resurgence of my coven and attempted to send word to those who still practice in my name. This act would have placed my followers, and most of all, Angélique, in grave danger. One of my guardians intercepted the message before it was discovered. While I feel Marguerite's intentions were good, I could not let this go unpunished.

Charles and Madeline, let Marguerite's death act as your first and only warning: tell no one of Angélique's origin and know I am always watching you.

The Lady of the Forest

Marguerite mulled over the letter and scratched her chin, her uneven yellow nails catching on her chin hair. Orion curled his lips in disgust at her unkempt appearance. She harrumphed at him, then stuck a finger in her ear and wiggled it around until he was forced to look away. "That will teach you," she mumbled. She asked him to repeat the ending lines of the letter, nodding a few times and muttering under her breath. "She did a very nice job," the old woman remarked aloud. "Please tell her I am impressed, but I do have a warning for her." Marguerite stared up at the tall Fae.

"And what is that?" His patience was wearing thin.

"I explained to her that my gift is unpredictable, but strong." Her cloudy eye glowed in the night, the milky light highlighting the hills and deepening the ravines of her face. Her voice was flat. "**The crown that sparkles and shines upon your head will soon feel like lead. A new line has begun, will never be undone. Your demise will come from a twisted prize: the one who carries the legacy of her mother's pain, licked by the flames, will come for the queen. Wait and—**" But the old woman never finished her prophecy.

There was a horrible gurgle as Orion slit the woman's throat, letting his emotions get the better of him. He would punish himself once the job was done for succumbing to his emotions. *How dare this human order him to threaten his lady!*

Orion transcribed the message in the old woman's blood as instructed. He placed her body on the stool on the front step, tilting her head downward since the cut he had made was very deep. Orion was unconcerned about visitors in this area of the woods, but just in case, the old woman would appear as though she was sleeping. He stepped back, resting his chin on his thumb, raking his eyes over the body. Knowing the scent of blood might attract wolves, he lit bonfires around the house's perimeter to keep any predators away until the morning. Then he ran back to the house and slipped the note under the door. The orange streaks of firelight lit up the darkness and would easily be seen from inside the house. Orion perched atop a tree and waited.

Charles was the first to burst out the front door. The note was clutched in his hand, his nightshirt half-tucked into his trousers. In his haste, he knocked the body off the stool and screamed. Madeline came running with the baby cradled in her arms. She dropped to her knees, clutching the child to her chest. Orion watched them read the note together and look at the body lying on the ground. The two gazed into the forest lit up by the bonfires, as if they were searching for something, anything—*anyone* who might be watching them. However, they would not find the person, or Fae, responsible for this.

Charles tucked the rest of his nightshirt into his pants and comforted his wife, then coaxed her back into the house. She stroked the baby in her arms and gave her grandmother a final glance. The man ran his hands through his hair, then dragged the body to one of the bonfires, tossing it on top. He made the sign of the cross and bowed his head.

Orion's job was complete.

Lady Sekhmet returned to her summer compound, waiting for word from Orion. She had not been able to finish speaking with Aurora, as the queen was napping again. *The queen had been doing that a lot lately*, Sekhmet noted.

Orion strode into the main hall, where his lady was prepping flowers to hang and dry for spells.

"My lady," Orion said with a bow.

"I take it there were no complications," Sekhmet said, as more of a confirmation than a question.

"The old woman has been disposed of, and the message was received by the human man and woman. I witnessed them reading it together." Orion's tone was flat; he braced for her to ask him for details, knowing he would have to tell her about the old woman's words.

"Anything else?"

"The woman had a message for you before her death."

Sekhmet chuckled, never taking herself away from the task at hand. "A message for me? Oh, this should be interesting. Please enlighten me."

Orion straightened. "The woman referred to her gift as unpredictable, but strong. Then she said the following, my lady: The crown that sparkles and shines upon your head will soon feel like lead. A new line has begun, will never be undone. Your demise will come from a twisted prize: the one who carries the legacy of her mother's pain, licked by the flames, will come for the queen. Wait and—"

Sekhmet's expression changed from amusement to fury, the flowers shrinking and wilting in her hand. "And what? Orion, *and*?"

"That was all she said, my lady."

Sekhmet set her flowers down. "Look what you made me do to my beautiful babies!" With a wave of her wrist, the peonies went from withering limp carcasses to spring blooms. Sekhmet squared her shoulders, teeth gritted. "Now what do you mean, that was all she said? She could not finish her statement or would not?" Her gaze zeroed in on her most trusted guard.

"I killed her before she finished her statement," he said coolly.

Lady Sekhmet's eyebrows rose for a moment. With a subtle flick of her wrist, vines shot out from the wall, wrapping around Orion's entire body and tethering him there. To his credit, he did not struggle. Sekhmet made a fist, and the vines tightened.

"I deserve your anger," he said.

"Yes, you do. You let your emotions control you, and I lost important information that I could have used. Your emotions do not come before logic! That is the Vila oath, is it not?"

"You are correct. Emotions do not control the Vila. Loyalty to the Lady of the House of Hathor before oneself. Always, my lady. Cleanse me of my mistake," he begged in a controlled whisper.

Sekhmet released the tension in her hands, the vines retracted, and Orion dropped to the floor. "You have learned your lesson," she said, regaining her composure.

Is That All There Is?

"Let us dissect the old woman's message and extrapolate what we can, because it sounds like we will have to keep an eye on this infant and what happens to her. It also implies this child is linked to who is going to be our next queen."

Chapter Seventeen:
One Last Speech

Aurora had convinced Lady Sekhmet to leave her alone just before she fell asleep, giving the queen time to gather her thoughts, especially after their philosophical discussion. *Serena would have enjoyed that conversation.* Aurora sighed at the thought of Serena. *None of this would be happening if you were here Serena.* She listened for the waves, but there was silence, shook her head, the mermaid was dead.

This was the last opportunity to ruminate before she put her plan into action. She had appreciated Sekhmet's company, but she needed the peace and quiet. Aurora also wanted a chance to grieve for everything she had lost, especially her daughter. Her child —a perfect little creature she had held for less than a few breaths yet captured her heart so readily—would never know her mother. The tears welled up again. Aurora knew she needed to be strong. The bishops, once known as *her* bishops, were ruthless Fae who had shed their skin and transformed into vipers right before her eyes. They plotted to have her meet

One Last Speech

her Oblivion simply because they did not agree with her beliefs regarding the Dark Fae. They were going to blame her death on an innocent Fae and send him and his kin to their Oblivion purely to quench their thirst for power. Dragor's words echoed in her head: "Lack of action leads to others' explosive reactions."

The signs had been there, but perhaps she had chosen to ignore them. She recalled how quickly Bishop Geddes had stepped into the role of senior bishop after Bishop Ingor met his Oblivion. How Bishop Geddes had given the approval to General Narcissi's plan for the Battle of Secor Valley without telling her the whole story. When she confronted Geddes about the loss of the ice dragons' young, he had shown no compunction. *Yes, the signs were there, and Dragor was correct: I did nothing.* She was not surprised Geddes was behind the plan to end her reign.

Aurora did find some solace in knowing she was going to use Geddes' plan against him and manipulate Fae law to protect Jarvok. Once an attempt was made on the life of a guest of the Court of Light, they were placed under the protective custody of the Illuminasqua until the predator was apprehended and their punishment upheld. With the elite warriors of her court watching over Jarvok, the bishops would not be able to make any moves against him or his kin. True, Jarvok would be upset with her, but she hoped the note would explain her motives. She did not look forward to stepping into the role of a villain, but there was no other way to avoid a fiery future. Dragor and Awynn had both asked her, "What are you willing to sacrifice for those you love?" At the time, she was not even sure she understood love, but after gazing at her child, seeing the life she and Jarvok had created together from one perfect aura-blending session, how could it be anything but love? The answer became so simple and uncomplicated. She was willing to sacrifice herself for them.

The mistakes of the past confused Aurora. In one sense, they seemed insignificant compared to what she faced now, but they also had led her to this situation.

Aurora was exhausted. Pretending to have root fever to hide the pregnancy until they could do the walk in spell had been difficult. Lady Sybella and her Familiar, Rowan, had tried to visit several times, but they had been turned away. Theadova had come every day to check on her, but he was refused an audience. Even Hogal had left a few notes. She had become a recluse, but she had no choice. Awynn needed to be able to speak with her whenever he had new information, and the Oracle and her Familiar somehow prevented that. The root fever lie covered up her gestational state and allowed Awynn free rein. What she had found amusing was that even though Bishop Geddes could have seen her, since as an Earth elemental he was immune to the illness, he had not come by at all in the past few weeks.

Now it was of no consequence. Tonight, she would address her kin for the first time in weeks. Lady Sekhmet had told the bishops their queen was cured. Queen Aurora would announce the Unity Contract signing to her kin and lay the foundation for her plan.

She donned her crown for what she knew would be the final time. Lady Sekhmet believed this would be cleared up quickly, and Aurora would be revered in the end, but deep down, the queen knew there was no coming back from this. She stared at the Fae looking back at her from the mirror. Aurora studied the red fire in her hair, the way her eyes

One Last Speech

held a cold turquoise flame. She was an inferno of love and hate intertwined in a fight for control of her very being. The love for her daughter and Jarvok was all-consuming, but the hatred for those who had forced her into giving it up burned hotter and more furiously. One was controlled and the other was chaos, which was exactly what she was: chaos waiting to be unleashed.

"You look magnificent," Awynn said in a low whisper.

Startled, Aurora turned to see her former bishop standing in the corner. "Thank you." She fixed a stray hair, tucking it behind her crown.

"The bishops have the fake Galena blade hidden in the solarium. What is your plan?" Awynn inquired.

Aurora squared her shoulders. "Tomorrow I will insist on Jarvok signing first. I asked that he draw up the contract since I conceded to all of his requests. I will make the announcement tonight to push Geddes and his minions over the edge. Once you tell me the bishops have planted the real Galena blade in Jarvok's suite, I will have Lady Sekhmet retrieve it. The fake blade with the liquid iron will be in the ceremonial box kept by the bishops."

Awynn pressed his thumb to his lips. "You will present the fake blade to Jarvok during the contract signing?"

She nodded. "I must tell you that Lady Sybella and Lady Zarya will be present. There was no way around it. Holly and Rowan will be there as well." Aurora knew Awynn had asked for them to be kept away.

"I will not be able to materialize."

Aurora nodded. "You understand this is protocol. I was unable to circumvent Fae law. I will ask Jarvok to sign first so Lady Sybella will read his intentions, which will keep me safe. Lady Zarya will never get a chance to read my intentions because it will go no further. I will personally hand Jarvok the knife. I know he will insist on his Elestial Blade, but because this is a Unity Contract, our blood must be drawn by the same blade. Jarvok will follow my lead. When I hand him the blade, I will drop the real blade from my gown, exposing the two identical Galena blades. At that point, I have to trust that Zion will presume that there has been an attempt on his king's life. Lady Sekhmet will insist on a thorough examination of the knife, where they will discover the liquid iron. I will be arrested and charged with attempted murder. Jarvok and his kin will be placed under protective custody. Once the bishops leave the room, Sekhmet will give him the letter I wrote explaining why I did it." Aurora took a deep breath after her detailed explanation.

"Well, it seems to me you have it all figured out. Let us hope you can protect the Fae you love better than—" Awynn stopped himself.

"Better than I protected you," Aurora finished for him.

Awynn bowed his head. "Go prepare for your speech, Your Grace." He placed his hands on her shoulders and kissed her cheek before dissolving into the ether. The guilt coating Awynn's parting words settled upon her shoulders like a heavy coat.

There was a knock on Aurora's door. "Come," she said abruptly. She had been feigning detachment from those she trusted to help convince them she was capable of attempted murder.

"Your Grace, are you ready?" Desdemona inquired, idling in the doorway.

"Yes."

One Last Speech

Desdemona caught the chill in the air. "The bishops are ready, as you requested."

Aurora rose, straightening her gown. Desdemona noticed this was not her queen's usual attire. Aurora's gown was avant garde, lacking the polished sophistication of the dresses she'd worn for other events. There were dark circles under her eyes, she had lost a considerable amount of weight, and her face was gaunt. Her high cheekbones appeared skeletal to Desdemona instead of regal. *It must be the root fever*, Desdemona thought. Except, Aurora emanated a certain energy, cold and closed-off.

The captain wanted to shake her queen and friend. Aurora had been acting this way for weeks, and all attempts to break through her icy facade had failed. Desdemona had been relegated to playing the quiet shadow. She knew it was not her job to judge Aurora—after all, the crown is heavy.

The captain of the Illuminasqua held the door open. Aurora glided through and strode toward the Great Hall without so much as a glance. "You should have your cape on tonight, Captain. This is a formal event," Aurora said as they walked side-by-side. Her tone was frank, chilly.

"I have it hanging near the platform. I shall put it on. I do apologize."

Aurora gave her a sideways glare. "See that you do before you announce me."

"Yes, Your Grace." Desdemona crinkled her brow. Her queen was never concerned about such things. Her uniform was something the bishops would nitpick, not Aurora.

As the two Fae entered the corridor leading to the Great Hall, Desdemona took the black cape hanging like liquid onyx from the hook. Aurora watched as Desdemona wrapped it around herself and clipped it to her left shoulder.

"Much better." Aurora tilted her chin, signaling for Desdemona to bring the meeting to order.

The captain of the Illuminasqua bowed and walked across the elevated platform with thunder in her steps. Desdemona commanded respect, and the room quieted when she came into view.

"Silence! Your queen has requested your presence and wishes to speak with all Fae. May I present: Queen Aurora," Desdemona announced in a booming voice. The crowd bowed their heads. The bishops stayed behind the throne as the queen entered the Great Hall.

Aurora stalked up the platform, her leg peeking between the pleats of her skirt. Her crown glittered in the firelight offered by the candelabra. A fleeting thought of Jarvok crossed her mind; she missed him terribly. But her steely resolve would crumble if he were standing beside her, given what lay before her. The queen gathered her courage with her shoulders back and her head held high. She looked majestic as she raised her arms up in greeting. "Merry meet, my kin," she called.

The crowd responded in a single chorus of "Merry meet."

Aurora gazed out into the crowd. Fae of all kinds met her eyes—some friendly, others inquisitive, and a few judgmental. She understood their emotional states. She also knew that her actions tomorrow would upset many of them, but acute discomfort would be better than prolonged pain. It would certainly be better than their inevitable Oblivion.

"Tomorrow will be a day of change for the Court of Light." She was careful with her words. She did not want to make promises she had no intention of keeping. "For those who are unsure about the changes, I offer these words: look

One Last Speech

to each other for solace, find comfort in your kin, borrow strength from one another, and know I have always looked out for you and will continue to do so."

The crowd remained stoic and quiet. Aurora gazed into the crowd, uneasy at their silence. Her speech was unrehearsed. She was speaking from the heart and hoped she was hitting the correct notes. *This is my final attempt at bringing the kingdom together before I tear it asunder.*

Aurora took a breath and finished her thoughts: "Though some of you may not agree with my methods or choices, I hope you understand they come from a place of love and light. We are all Fae: Light or Dark, Power or Virtue. We all comprehend the language of compassion. To alienate our kin who were born to do a job that some deem beneath them is to hold on to antiquated beliefs. Beliefs we need to abandon as we were abandoned. The Dark Fae started their lives out as Angels, just as we did. They were left here on Earth, just as we were. They made their share of mistakes, just as we have. Yet, we judge them more harshly than we judge ourselves. Why? Because we were taught their old responsibilities made them submissive to us as Virtues. Their job was to protect and sacrifice, which is one of the most honorable gifts one can give another. Why should they not be revered?"

There were whispers and nods of agreement.

"Regardless of who rules this palace, Dark and Light are just labels. We are all Fae. Remember what *Fae* means: the Fellowship Aegis of Earth. A fellowship is a group of equals brought together for a purpose: we protect the Earth and each other. I will do anything to protect you—remember that even when it seems I have gone against the very things I speak of now. I am always protecting you. In the words of a Fae more enlightened than I: 'compassion is a universal language, one that transcends all factions.' We must be generous with it. We do not always know what hurt another is carrying to make them act the way they do, so use compassion as your lens instead of judgment. Understand not everything is what it seems, my kin."

Aurora looked toward the bishops as she spoke the last line. Bishop Geddes did not flinch, nor did Ward, but Caer turned away, unable to meet her eyes. Aurora was greeted with applause from the crowd. She smiled, and hot tears pricked at her eyes. The crowd exuded anxious energy, excitement, and hope. She understood that part of what she had said would seem hypocritical in hindsight, but she hoped many would see through the shroud of her words. She hoped her message would be taken to heart. That way when Jarvok took the throne, they would give him the respect he deserved.

Chapter Eighteen:
NERVES

In the visitors' suite, Jarvok reviewed the Unity Contract with Lady Zarya and Holly. It was their tenth time reading it, according to Zion's estimation.

"What in Lucifer's name is he so nervous about?" Zion whispered to Asa, who was busy studying a tapestry depicting a meteor striking Earth. Tiny, green crystal flecks caught her eye. They looked like emerald, yet they hummed with power as she waved her hand over them.

Asa ignored Zion's question and commented on the tapestry instead. "They used moldavite crystal to represent what they now know was King Jarvok when he fell back to Earth. I have heard the Light Fae regard moldavite as the best representation of the Fae—the celestial and terrestrial melding to become one, a unique fusion. Perhaps this would be the perfect crystal for the centerpiece of his new crown."

Zion rolled his eyes. "Yeah, yeah, pretty green crystal. 'I'm Asa, I am *so* knowledgeable about *rocks*, look at me!' Now can you please answer me? Because our king is acting like a long-tailed troll in a room full of rocking chairs." Zion physically turned Asa in Jarvok's direction, his hands on her shoulders.

She let out a long hissing exhale at her best friend. "Really, Zion? You can be so immature. I will not read him. He did not ask me to, and I am not to go where I am not invited. Need I remind you what happened last time? I will not violate his trust." She shook his hands off her shoulders.

Zion did recall the last time Asa had inadvertently read her king's mind. She revealed he had never aura-blended with another Fae. Embarrassed, Jarvok had become enraged and threatened to throw her in the pit if she ever read him again without permission. Zion had stepped in to spare her.

Zion put his arms around her shoulders, hugging her for a moment. Then he stroked her long hair below her helmet. Asa rarely took her helmet off, and he had not seen her with her mask off since before the war. He knew the scars on her face had worsened. But he smiled at how much her hair had grown. "Your hair has gotten so long. I remember when it was only as long as a Will-o-Wisp's wing, and now it is well past your shoulders."

She turned her head slightly. "Sweet-talking won't work, Zion, but I can tell you that Jarvok is not nervous. He is scared. I don't have to read his mind to see that—it's as plain as day."

Zion paused for a second with his fingers intertwined in her hair. "You have different shades of blue now: light blue, a little bit of turquoise mixed in with the white streaks, and even royal blue," he observed, twirling the strands to see the hues blend. "It's very pretty. So, why do you think he is scared?" Zion picked up a handful of hair and let it cascade through his hands, transfixed.

Asa knew what he was doing, but she also knew he was genuinely concerned for their king. She still was not going to read their king without his permission. She moved her head forward, gently releasing her hair from Zion's fingers. "I do not know why exactly he is scared. Nor whether his fears are based in his heart or in his head. I will only say fear is rolling off him. If you want to help him, keep his mind busy so he does not focus on those fears," Asa said, turning to face him.

Zion put his hands up in surrender. "All right, I understand, no more pushing." He winked at her.

She watched Zion approach Jarvok. He feigned an interest in the Unity Contract, asking questions and engaging the king. Asa felt herself smiling, thinking he would make a good leader someday. But the smile soon faded as a cold tingle crept up her spine. The thought of Zion being a good leader wasn't the issue; she had a sense that things were about to change. *Something* had been set into motion and they were all about to be swept up in the riptide. "Chaos be with us," she whispered.

Chapter Nineteen:
All My Loath and Blight Upon You

Aurora paced in her chambers as she awaited word from Lady Sekhmet that she had obtained the Galena dagger. She did not know how Sekhmet was going to get the dagger from the suite, but her friend did not seem too concerned when asked to complete the task. Trying to keep herself busy, Aurora fixed her long, wavy ponytail. It cascaded down her back in stunning contrast to the white dress. She painted her lips a deep purple in honor of Jarvok. "Traitor" whispered in her head. That is what Jarvok would call her.

She smoothed her gown, feeling slightly uncomfortable in the white lace ensemble. The dress was sleeveless, with a V-neckline highlighting her décolletage. The silhouette hugged her every curve The ivy embroidery covered all the right areas, while the nude illusion made it appear as though the queen was draped in nothing but white lace. All she was waiting to put on was the belted bustle made of tiered silk tulle. The train of the skirt was over three feet long, but it was not a fashion statement; it was a necessity. Awynn had suggested the outfit, to help throw the bishops off their game. They still believed she was pregnant. Aurora did not appear as if she was with child in the painted-on dress, with every curve of her body on full display. Her left hand lingered over her lower belly, and Aurora glanced down; Sekhmet said she would bleed by the new moon, more symbolic of the success of the walk in spell. There was a pang of guilt that one life's journey had to end for her child to survive. Still, while Aurora had basic respect for life, she would kill for her child to live. The soul had made its choice, and all she had done was take advantage of that.

Aurora was still having reservations about today. She had reconsidered going through with her plan to betray Jarvok. However, every time she thought about telling him, Awynn appeared and reminded her why that plan would not work. She knew he was right. This was a situation that could lead to an explosive reaction. Aurora still had questions for Awynn. After today, Jarvok and her daughter would be safe, but how this would stop the bishops from stealing Awynn's essence, she did not understand. When she asked him, he told her that once she was neutralized as a risk, they would no longer need him and would release him to his Oblivion. Aurora did not believe it would be that easy. Awynn was optimistic about the situation; it was who he was.

A rhythmic knock came from outside Aurora's door. "Yes?"

Orion, Sekhmet's guard, responded. "Your Grace, I have a message from my lady for you. May I enter?"

Aurora opened the door for him with a flick of her wrist, asking the wind to assist her. When the door opened, the tall, muscular Fae stood in the entryway. The gold of his pauldrons glittered as the sunlight shone through the stained glass in the hall. "Orion, please come in." Aurora had dealt with enough of the Vila Faction to know they were very literal. They liked structure and did not assume anything; just because you opened a door for them did not mean they would walk through it. You had to grant them permission.

Orion bowed and entered.

Aurora closed the door behind him with another turn of her wrist. "Do you have a message for me from your lady?" she asked, understanding they were conversing in code, making sure to place a special emphasis on the word *message*.

Orion nodded and produced a long gold box. "My lady says she wishes you well in your endeavor, and she believes the universe will guide you to your target." He pivoted and left the room without another sound.

Aurora waited until he cleared the door to close it behind him. Then she removed the foil cover of the box, carefully unwrapping the lilac silk holding the authentic Galena dagger. She hugged the blade to her chest as a sigh of relief escaped her lips. "Thank you, Sekhmet," Aurora whispered, pressing her plum-colored lips to the blade.

The queen went to her gilded mirror and put on the final piece to her ensemble. She clicked the crystal-encrusted belt around her waist and fluffed the tulle skirt trailing behind her. Then with great care, she tucked the dagger into the belt at her right hip, using the tulle to hide the blade. Aurora checked herself in the mirror one last

All My Loath and Blight Upon You

time, glancing at her crown upon the dressing table. She did not need it. Today, she did not see herself as a queen. She was a lover protecting the one she loved. Bareheaded, she stood at her door, squeezing her eyes shut. "Forgive me, Jarvok, all my love and light," she whispered.

Jarvok, his lieutenants, and the High Council Guard gathered in the Great Hall. A table with the Unity Contract lay waiting, with the bishops' special Galena blade next to the parchment. All that was missing were the signatures of the leaders of each court. The bishops were present, along with the Oracles and their familiars. Dragor stood in the corner as the representative of the Draconian Faction.

Today, the Draconian Faction would be officially recognized and named a royal house by decree. This would give the dragons a voice in the Court of Light. The Draconians would enjoy the duality of both Light and Dark, since technically, they were not Fae. This was a show of respect. It was Aurora's way of making up, in small part, for the Battle of Secor Valley.

The Ice-Breathers, Acid-Breathers, and Fire-Breathers would each choose a leader to represent the secondary houses, with Dragor as the head of the royal house for the entire Faction. Jarvok suggested the possibility of the representatives being the leaders of the Draconians' special forces. Aurora shivered when he mentioned the Blaze Battalion, given her premonitions. However, Dragor could chose whichever dragons he deemed fit. This agreement was originally part of King Jarvok's terms during the Unity negotiations, but Aurora had suggested it be made into a decree; this way it was not contingent upon their Unity Contract. The Draconians saw this as a symbol of good faith and agreed to it. Now all that was required was for Dragor to sign it, or more accurately, to leave his mark.

No one escorted Aurora to the Great Hall. However, the queen insisted Desdemona take a few of her best Illuminasqua and station them within the Hall in case rebels tried to disrupt the signing. Desdemona did not argue, a rare occurrence that Aurora chalked up to her frosty demeanor toward her captain. It seemed Desdemona did not take liberties with her queen when they were on these colder terms.

Aurora entered the hall without fanfare, but once Jarvok laid eyes on her, it was as though they were the only two Fae in the kingdom. He pushed past his kin to greet Queen Aurora, who extended her arms to him. "Your Grace, how are you feeling?" He took her hands in his and kissed each one softly. He examined her pallor, scanning for any signs of the illness that had kept them apart.

She smiled, demurely tilting her head downward. A rosy blush colored her cheeks. "Merry meet. I am well, King Jarvok. Your correspondence was very much appreciated during my recovery. I thank you. I enjoyed Los very much."

She turned to the room and gave a general acknowledgment to the Fae in attendance. Her brow furrowed a moment when she did not see Lady Sekhmet.

King Jarvok, ever observant, caught the passing expression on his beloved's face. "What ails you?"

Aurora waved it off. "I was expecting Lady Sekhmet to be here, but I see she is running late. No matter, we can begin and have Dragor seal the decree regarding the

Draconian Faction," the queen said, eager to complete one last task before her reign's abrupt end.

The bishops all shifted uncomfortably at her words. Awynn's voice floated into her mind. "Do not let them disrespect you, my queen. They seek to destroy you."

"Problem, Bishop Geddes?" Aurora was no longer concerned with protocol or decorum, given he was one of the factors that had driven her to this moment.

The other two bishops backed up from their cohort, unable to hide their surprise at the queen's brashness.

Geddes straightened and fidgeted with his cape. "No, Your Grace, not at all. I applaud your generous gesture to the dragons."

"I did not ask for your opinion, Bishop Geddes. If I want your opinion, I will give it to you." Aurora scoffed.

Standing behind Zion in formation, Yagora and Pria chuckled at Aurora's scolding of her senior advisor. Asa's mask shifted as her eyebrows practically hit her hairline. Zion exchanged a glance with Asa, prodding her with his eyes. However, Asa was not about to go where she was not invited.

Holly and Rowan immediately felt the fur on the back of their necks stand straight up. The Oracles stroked them, sensing their Familiars' anxiety rise. An unspoken conversation passed between all four. They sensed something was happening. Aurora was not acting like herself; she was on guard, lashing out, and there was darkness around her aura.

Rowan sniffed the air, and his eyes went wide as Queen Aurora glided past them. "Holly, I do believe we have a relative who has paid us a visit," Rowan mumbled to the mink in a subdued voice, his proper English accent thick with worry.

Holly's eyes narrowed, and she dropped her head in defeat. "Yes, Rowan, I think one of our cousins has made the Court of Light their new home. This is going to get very messy." The mink shook her head.

The Oracles put their hands on each other's shoulders. "Zarya, did you feel the air change?" Lady Sybella asked.

"Yes. I recognized it like the sun setting. A coldness is following the queen. She feels as if she is walking in the dark, like on a moonless night. There is no light," Zarya replied.

"Why does the Dark Fae empath not say anything? Surely she must know what is going on?" Sybella inquired.

Zarya subtly shook her head, her black hair with its mint-green streaks dancing over her silver skin. "No, she is disconnected from her abilities while she wears her armor. She must choose to use them and drop her shields. Her king has reprimanded her for reading him without his permission. She views Aurora as his equal. She will not."

Seeking comfort, Zarya stroked Holly and Sybella did the same with Rowan. They did not know what was about to happen, but they were aware it was out of their control. All they could do was prepare for the aftermath.

Jarvok smiled at his queen. He enjoyed seeing this more aggressive side of her. In a way, he hoped it was his influence helping her to be more authoritative with the bishops. He had never trusted them, except for the Fire Drake Awynn.

"Dragor," Jarvok invited the black dragon to the table.

Aurora nodded, and a copper brand was brought to the table, bearing a new Fae sigil. "This parchment states the Draconian Faction is, now and forever, from this moment onward, a royal house of the Court of Light. It gives the Draconian Faction duality in both the Court of

Light and the Court of Dark. You will have full privileges as a member of both courts. Dragor is named as Head of the House of Draconian. He will be the representative and will have a say in all matters concerning your faction. The Ice-Breathers, Acid-Breathers, and Fire-Breathers will be secondary houses with their own representatives. We understand your loyalty is to your faction first. Please accept this as an acknowledgment of being an honorary Fae and know this is to prevent another tragedy like what transpired at the Battle of Secor Valley. I cannot undo the past, and for that my heart is heavy. This is merely a step toward bridging the gap and building upon a new understanding." Aurora bowed her head as she held the copper pole out to him. "You have been given your faction's symbol; please use your fire to heat the brand and seal the agreement."

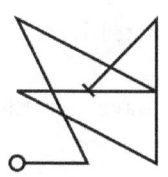

Draconian Sigil

Dragor clicked his back teeth, and the fire plating around his neck flared out as the dragon sharply inhaled. He exhaled, and a concentrated stream of purple fire lit up the room. The copper sparked blue and white, and then Dragor placed the brand on the parchment next to Aurora's seal. The room erupted into cheers, and Dragor bowed his head.

The parchment floated up, and the Oracles placed their hands on it, sealing the decree. *"As it is above, so it is below, so mote it be. What is done can never be undone. This decree was completed with the utmost of true intentions. It is upheld and filed into Fae history. The Draconians are the fifth royal house to join the Court of Light, so mote it be. Hail and welcome, Dragor, Head of the House of Draconian."* The Oracles' voices rang out in unison as the parchment lit up and disappeared into the depths of the Fae archives.

King Jarvok was the first to hug his dragon, who looked very pleased with himself. Dragor turned to Aurora and bent his head to the queen, but she said nothing, for what was coming next took all the goodness from her heart.

"Now we sign the Unity Contract, and we may continue in celebration!" King Jarvok's voice was jubilant as he focused on Aurora. "My queen, after you." Jarvok led her to the table.

"No, please, you first, I insist," Aurora said, handing him the Galena blade.

"Oh, my dear, I have my Elestial Blade." Jarvok unsheathed his Auric weapon.

Geddes smiled.

Aurora caressed Jarvok's arm. "We must both use the same blade, as it is a Unity Contract. I would prefer if we shared the Galena blade, King Jarvok," she purred into his ear.

"Your Grace, if King Jarvok would prefer to use hi—" Bishop Geddes protested.

Aurora's energy wings practically exploded from her back in a blinding fuchsia glow. "You dare to question me?" She sent the bishop flying backward with a gust of wind. "It is my Unity Contract. I will have it signed as I see fit."

Then she turned back toward Jarvok, her tone sugar-sweet. "The Galena blade, please, my liege."

Upon hearing "my liege," Zion's head tilted up, his eyes narrowing on the Light Fae queen. *Her dress is kind of tight for Aurora. I mean not that I am complaining, but like really tight. Nice ass. If Jarvok ever heard me say that, he would skin me alive. But her eyes... the circles under them—has she slept at all?—and she has lost weight; this could all be due to the root fever, I guess,* he thought. He shrugged but something was still gnawing at him. *While she was short-tempered, the bishops were annoying. Still, in my time around her, I have never heard her refer to Jarvok as "my liege."* In fact, she deliberately dances *around using the phrase to address the king.*

As she handed Jarvok the blade, something like bugs crawling over Zion's skin caused him to leap forward. "Wait, my liege!" he found himself yelling, though he did not know why.

Lady Sekhmet barged into the room as well. "Your Grace, I am sorry for my tardiness."

Sekhmet's late arrival and Zion's outburst startled Aurora, causing her to stumble back. A metal ping against the floor echoed throughout the Great Hall. A blade danced on the floor for what seemed like an eternity. Everyone watched, transfixed, as the shiny object teeter-tottered back and forth on the quartz floor, ringing out like an alarm bell. For Zion, that was exactly what it was. Acting on instinct, he grabbed the other blade out of his king's hand. Jarvok looked intensely at Aurora.

Desdemona dropped from the ceiling to break the spell. The captain of the Illuminasqua picked up the Galena blade from the floor and rushed to Zion. "May I examine that blade?" Zion handed it to her without hesitation. Desdemona did not turn away; she wanted Zion to see her inspect it. Aurora dropped her head, avoiding Jarvok's gaze. Desdemona checked the tip of the blade Zion had given her, then pressed her finger to it; her flesh sizzled. She found the mechanism meant to inject the liquid iron. "Pure iron. With a hidden apparatus to inject liquid iron into the bloodstream," she said, eyeing her inflamed, blistering skin.

The bishops exchanged uneasy glances. Caer elbowed Ward, but Geddes stopped them both with one fierce look. *Let's see how this plays out*, he thought. *We can debate how Aurora found the extra blade later.*

Zion locked eyes with Aurora and lunged for her. "*You!* This was a setup! You were going to kill him!"

Desdemona threw him back with one hand. "Control him," she warned Asa.

Asa shook her head, seething. "Why? He is correct. Your queen is a liar."

Desdemona stalked over to Aurora. "My queen, now is the time to speak." The captain glanced around, aware of the tension mounting in the room.

Geddes' grip tightened on his staff. The scent of wet moss grew around him as he gathered his energy. He knew that if Aurora was going to implicate them, now would be the time.

Aurora scowled at Jarvok. "I did." Her voice remained steady. "My kin were against this union. Hostility has been building for several weeks. Fae are turning against each other. I had to protect those I love the most. This was my only option. I did try to kill King Jarvok by switching the Galena blade. I waive my right to a trial by my kin.

Take me and place the king in protective custody with the Illuminasqua. He and his kin are still in danger from my sympathizers, and by Fae law he is to be protected until my punishment is enacted."

Confused, Geddes began to call his power back. *What is she doing? Perhaps she didn't know our plan? Or perhaps she was just that sloppy.*

Desdemona sighed. "Illuminasqua, you have been called." Ten female forms of identical height and build dressed in black vests and pants fell from the sky, their dark hoods covering their hair. "Take the queen to the cells." It took four of the ten elite Fae warriors to bind the queen with her hands behind her back and her ankles in black onyx shackles. Aurora, to her credit, did not struggle. The other six stayed at attention, hands on the pearly grips of their Harbingers swords, braced for a showdown with the Dark Fae.

Once bound, Aurora was escorted past Jarvok, who put his hand up, halting the parade of shame. She stiffened, prepared for his wrath.

"Was it all a lie?" he asked in a hushed voice.

She swallowed. Awynn had prepared her for the question. He had told her to make it believable, or else she would be risking Jarvok's life. "Yes." Her eyes were cold and emotionless.

Jarvok's jaw ticked. "All my loath and blight upon you, Aurora," he snarled as she was ushered past.

Geddes gave a subtle nod to the other bishops, who remained quiet. *Either Aurora was a better actress than we expected*, Geddes thought, *or she did our job for us. Either way, our problem may be solved.*

Zion snarled at Aurora's answer, but Asa was struggling, her fists clenched. Asa wanted to delve into Aurora's emotions and find out what was going on, but Jarvok did not give her the command to do so, and whatever she found out, she would have to report. Asa glanced at Jarvok, whose heartbreak was obvious. She did not want to make it worse for him, but when she focused on the disgraced queen, it was clear Aurora was hiding something. Asa just didn't know what.

Desdemona addressed the Dark Fae as a collective: "You are under protective custody and are not to leave the Court of Light." She tried to sound sympathetic.

"The hell we are!" Zion stepped up to her. "You heard your lying troll of a queen! Our king is at risk."

Lady Sekhmet interjected, "Lieutenant Zion, King Jarvok, I cannot imagine your state of mind right now." She turned to Desdemona. "May I speak with them privately, Captain?"

Desdemona shook her head.

"Please, they have been through so much. It is the least we can do," Sekhmet said in a caring tone.

Desdemona looked at the Dark Fae. "Only if the others wait with me over there in the corner."

Jarvok nodded to his Fae, and they walked away with Desdemona, leaving Zion, Jarvok, and Sekhmet to speak. Dragor remained as well. No one was going to dare tell him otherwise given the circumstances.

"If I may," Sekhmet said carefully, "Queen—I mean, *Aurora*—waived her right to a trial. She will be executed swiftly, and as the victim, you will choose her mode of execution, but she is a Virtue so that does change things. I guess you will choose her executioner. Because only an

All My Loath and Blight Upon You

Elestial Blade will send her to her Oblivion." Sekhmet waved her hand. "I can speak with the bishops about having you come back on that day if it would please you. I would think you would want to leave the Court of Light and gather your thoughts in a more concealed manner. Oh, and I do have this letter that Aurora asked me to give to you, but now I am not sure." She held it out, but Jarvok hesitated. The cream-colored envelope appeared like a coiled viper, innocuous enough if left alone.

Dragor snorted, his eyes fixed on Zion.

Zion did not need any more of a prompt. He was in front of his king in a pixie's wingbeat, snatching it from Sekhmet before Jarvok could make his choice.

"Wait, what if it is enchanted?" Sekhmet's hand went to her mouth.

Zion threw the envelope up in the air and yelled, "*Uro!*" meaning "incinerate. The dragon wasted no time in clicking his back teeth, and a ribbon of purple, white, and green poured from his mouth as his fire plates compressed against his neck. The heat was controlled, and in less than five seconds, there wasn't even a pile of ash for Jarvok to look over.

Jarvok turned to his kin. "We are leaving the court of lies. We will return when the queen of betrayal is to meet her Oblivion."

The bishops ran out too, no doubt making plans for the exchange of power, unconcerned with the Dark Fae.

Chapter Twenty:
Help Me to Help You to Help Me...

Rowan crept through the corridors leading to the black onyx cells beneath the palace. He was on all four legs; he would switch to a bipedal stance once he arrived at his destination. The torches hanging on the walls cast a small amount of light. Most of it was swallowed up by the thick, black crystal rock. Over five hundred torches lit his way, yet they only provided a soft glow, allowing a Fae to see a mere five feet in front of them. Rowan's eyesight was impeccable despite the limited illumination, so he had no issues traversing the uneven stairs or the dips in the winding hallway.

Ahead, two Royal Guards waited at attention in front of a cell door. Rowan's mouth turned up; his informant had not been wrong. He stood upright. The guards were Finn and Riker—Fae of questionable character, known to frequent establishments specializing in gratifying bodily desires.

Help Me to Help You to Help Me...

Rowan fixed his green plume hat. He flicked it with his claws, checked his canteen to make sure it was full of plum sugar wine, straightened his back, and began whistling and skipping as he rounded the corner.

The guards immediately drew their spears, pointing them in the fox's direction. "Halt!"

"Hello, chaps. Riker and Finn, so nice to see you again." Rowan smiled ear to ear, his whiskers twitching.

The guards eyed each other until finally one guard blinked and the other lowered his spear. "Familiar Rowan. I am sorry, but you're not allowed to see Quee—um, Aur—the prisoner. By order of the bishops, she is not to have any visitors." The tall blond Fae with small ribbed brown horns protruding from the top of his helmet was Finn. His horns would grow to be almost a quarter the size of his body, arching backward. The distinct horn shape let Rowan know he was a member of the Capra Faction, and the size told him that Finn was not yet strong enough to hold a position of power in his own faction, and thus, he had entered the guard.

"Oh no, you misunderstand my intentions for this call, my friend. I am not here for the traitor, I am here for you, gentlefae." The fox flashed a toothy grin.

"Us?" the guard with the bluish-green complexion asked.

This would be Riker, Rowan thought, taking in the telltale complexion of the Algae Faction. *Not the brightest of all the factions, perfect!* "Well, of course, Guard Riker. You are both saddled with such an important job, and I am sure it has been forever since the two of you have seen the light of the sun. I thought I would bring you some good tidings. I have plum sugar wine to help you pass the time." Rowan showed them his canteen and began to pour them a cup.

"I thought perhaps you could use a break and see a friendly, albeit furry, face." Rowan held the cup out to Riker.

"No!" Finn replied with authority, stopping Riker from taking the wine.

"No?" Rowan repeated, hurt by the rejection.

"We are on duty," Finn reminded his cohort, turning his nose up. Rowan could see the fight in Finn's eyes. He was trying to resist temptation.

Rowan ran his paw over his whiskers. "How foolish of me! You are most honorable Fae—look at the job they have given you. They would not trust just any guards to do this. Only the most trustworthy and strong could complete this mission. Of course, you would never partake in libations, which could lead to a state of inebriation, altering your consciousness. My mistake, please forgive me." Rowan put his head down, feigning self-admonishment. He peeked up through his eyelashes to see Riker clearly lost in the fox's large vocabulary. His eyebrows were so close together they were practically kissing. Finn tried to hide his befuddlement by wiggling his finger in his ear and inspecting his findings.

Rowan poured the wine out onto the floor as the guards not so subtly licked their lips. "Being of such high moral fiber, I am sure neither of you would be interested in taking my place at Miss Trish's House of Trixx. I was supposed to have a date this evening, but Lady Sybella has called me to her side, and as her Familiar, I am bound to heed her call. The worst part is my time was with Miss Trish herself." Rowan kicked a pebble on the ground and stuck his paws behind his back for dramatic effect. He puffed his cheeks out, and his black nose twitched, adding to his look of disappointment. His whiskers waggled.

Help Me to Help You to Help Me...

Finn dropped his spear along with his bottom lip. "Did you say you were able to get time with *The Miss Trish*?" His voice dripped with envy at the idea of alone time with the infamous human brothel owner.

Rowan took off his green hat and held it to his chest. "Why, yes! Do you know Miss Trish?" His head tilted to the side and his ears perked up a bit. Not giving the guard time to answer, he continued. "Oh, what am I saying?" He placed his paw to his forehead. "Of course, such brave and noble Fae like yourselves know of her charming company. I am sure you have spent hours in her presence. We all know how wonderful that is, do we not? Why, she must melt when you enter her establishment. She probably clears her night for you both." Rowan smiled devilishly.

Finn and Riker exchanged a glance.

Rowan exhaled. "Well, my friends, this has been a lovely chat. When you see Miss Trish, tell her I am sorry for standing her up twice. I think she will be very angry with me. I must be on my way." Rowan put his hat on and picked up his canteen.

"Twice?" Finn asked.

"Oh, yes. I introduced Miss Trish to a Sanskrit text from India which helped her, how shall I say it? Gain a new perspective for her establishment. Her business has tripled, and she offered me two nights to explore the text together. Golly, I really hate to miss that. Well, good day, chaps!" Rowan did not get even two steps away before he heard his name being frantically called.

"Wait! Familiar Rowan! Please wait!" Finn yelled, his voice full of desperation.

Rowan quickly erased all traces of his smirk before he turned to reveal a somber expression. "Yes, my friends, did you need something of me?"

Finn rubbed the tip of his left horn. "Did you say you have the time already reserved with Miss Trish?" The guard bent down to one knee so he was eye level with the five-foot-tall fox.

"I did, my friend, but as I said, I am afraid she will take this as a personal insult when I do not show, and I will fall out of favor with the lovely Miss Trish." Rowan's shoulders slumped, and he sighed to punctuate his predicament.

Finn glanced over his shoulder at Riker, who jutted his chin toward his partner. "Well, familiar Rowan, perhaps we can help you."

Rowan's ears stuck straight up. "Help me, to help you, to help me?"

"Um... yeah..." Finn replied, confusion ghosting across his face as he tried to follow the fox's logic.

"How?" Rowan's eyes were wide and full of hope.

Finn leaned in and put his hand on the fox's shoulder. "We could take your place and help you save face with Miss Trish, as long as this stays between us." Finn motioned with his finger and winked.

"We will even pay for your time!" Riker added. Finn gave Riker a nasty look, which Rowan pretended not to notice.

Rowan rubbed his chin as if he were contemplating the plan. "But you are both on duty. Won't they know one of you is missing? I would hate myself if helping me got one of you in trouble."

Finn made a nonchalant gesture. "We are allowed breaks, and we can cover for each other."

Help Me to Help You to Help Me...

"Besides, you are the only visitor we have had," Riker said with a big smile.

Rowan was surprised at that, but he did not show it. "Well, that settles it. On one condition..." Rowan held out a small rolled-up piece of parchment with a pink seal bearing the letters "MT" within a small heart. The wax was a light pink like the color of spring tulips. Both guards recognized it as Miss Trish's personal insignia, and their mouths practically watered at the seal. Finn reached for it, but Rowan pulled it away, "I said I had a condition. You don't have to pay me back, just show Miss Trish a nice time and enjoy yourselves," the fox said, and the guards looked at each other.

"That's it?" Finn asked suspiciously.

"That is all, my friend. Oh, and I will bring the second invitation for Riker tomorrow night, so I can hear all about your time." Rowan winked at Finn.

Riker furrowed his brow at the last part of Rowan's statement. "How did you know I was going to go tomorrow night?"

Rowan smirked. "Just a hunch, my friend, you seem like the type who would let his best buddy go first." Riker smiled, and the fox went on. "You do know where her establishment is, chaps, correct?"

The two guards giggled like human courtiers. "Yes, familiar Rowan, thank you!"

"No, thank *you*. I shall return tomorrow's eve to hear all about your adventures, Guard Finn!" Rowan tipped his hat and walked away, whistling.

Once he was far enough away and he could no longer hear the guards whooping and hollering, Rowan whispered, "Like shooting trolls under a bridge."

A voice responded in his head. "Your job is not yet done, my Familiar," Lady Sybella reminded him.

"Yes, my lady, but 'tis close. I shall see you shortly to plan the next part," Rowan replied without saying a word aloud. He skipped up the stairs, self-satisfaction leading the way.

True to his word, Rowan returned the following evening to give Riker his invitation for time with Miss Trish. He was greeted by a very happy Finn and an impatient Riker. Finn was grateful for what he described as "a fun evening, one that I shall never forget." Rowan was positive Riker had heard the more explicit version, which explained why the other guard was practically crawling the walls while he waited for his turn. Rowan did not torture him any longer, and Riker cradled the parchment with the pale pink seal as if it were the Holy Grail itself. He hugged the fox and scampered off. Rowan smiled and told Finn he would return in a night or two to hear all of the details. Finn thanked Rowan for his generosity, and the familiar bid the guard adieu with a tip of his green hat, whistling a tune as he left the dungeon.

Two evenings later, when Rowan returned to see his friends in the dark onyx crystal cells, he was met with an overwhelming welcome. The smile on Riker's face said it all. The guards were beaming, and they were very gracious to the fox, taking every opportunity to express their gratitude.

Rowan made small talk with them, and when the moment was right, he pulled out a deck of cards. "How about it, my friends? Can I interest you in a game?" He

Help Me to Help You to Help Me...

shuffled the deck, letting the cards fly from one paw to the other, dazzling the guards with his tricks.

The guards grabbed their stools. "Deal me in, fox!" Finn demanded.

Rowan rattled off the rules of the Spanish card game Primero. "Three cards will be dealt to each of you, my dear Fae, and you place your bets on your hand. Any questions?"

"We know how to play Primero, fox, now deal," Finn replied.

Rowan paused for a second. "My, you are well-traveled. Few know the game. I am impressed, Finn. You must tell me of your jaunts."

Riker shook his head. "I don't smoke those, just these." He pulled out three sage and tobacco cigars.

Finn and Rowan glanced at each other and started to laugh at Riker's comment but caught themselves. "You are a fine Fae, Riker," Rowan said.

Riker frowned at the cigars. "But I only smoke when I drink and play cards," he said.

"Well, there *I* can help *you*..." Rowan smirked, shaking his canteen. "I know last time you honorable Fae said no, but..."

"Pour the wine, fox!" Riker said, and Rowan tipped his head. He passed the cups out to the guards and placed a cigar in his mouth.

Hours passed as the Fae and the fox drank, played cards, and shared stories about their exploits at Miss Trish's establishment, where the two Fae had thoroughly enjoyed themselves. As the evening drew to a close, the guards had lost most of their gold to Rowan. Yet, they were so inebriated; neither noticed the scope of their losses.

Rowan had enjoyed his share of plum sugar wine. "Well—*hic*—my Frae fiends—*hic*—no, that is not right..." Rowan waved his finger as the guards laughed.

"You are *dunk*," Finn said, giggling.

"It would disappear, I mean, appear... I is..." Rowan was chuckling too. The two guards nodded in agreement, using their spears to support themselves. "I can't go back to Lady Sybelly... Jady Yebe—the 'racle lad—like this..."

The guards shook their heads, trying not to fall.

Rowan swayed on his feet as he pointed at the pair. "Hey, you twos got a pretty good idea. I will stay—*hiccup*—here and sleep it off."

Finn smiled and slapped his knee, almost falling. "I *am* brilliant," he exclaimed.

"Yes, we are," Riker agreed.

"Okay, I am going to go to bed like you two just said, so no one sees me and you don't get in trouble. Boy, you guys are smart." Rowan patted Finn's cheek and turned toward the cell door they guarded.

"Wait!" Finn shouted.

The fox halted with his paw upon the cell door handle. "Oh, I—*hiccup*—almost forgot." Rowan wandered over to Finn, who appeared as though he was trying to remember why he had told the fox to stop in the first place. Rowan stretched up on his hind legs as tall as he could, still swaying, and beckoned the guard to lean down. When Finn obliged him, Rowan planted a wet kiss on the guard's cheek and smiled. "I forgot to give you a goodnight kiss... silly fox. Good night, buttercup," Rowan said.

Finn blushed. "Good night, fox," he said, and fell asleep right where he landed on the floor.

Riker pouted. "Me too!" He pointed to his cheek.

Help Me to Help You to Help Me...

Rowan staggered over to the other Fae. "Yes, you too, sweet pea... good night." Rowan kissed the guard on his cheek. "Sweet pea, could you open the door for me? But like *you* said, keep it unlocked so I can slip out before morning." Riker nodded and stumbled over to unlock the door for Rowan. The fox hugged the guard's leg. "Thanks, sweet pea."

The guard patted the fox's back, mumbling, "Love ya, Rowan." He promptly slid down the wall, fast asleep.

Rowan slipped into the cell, carefully closing the heavy door behind him. He put his ear to the door and listened for the guards' snoring patterns to even out before he spoke. "Your Grace? It is I, Rowan. Are you awake?" he whispered into the darkened cell.

Chapter Twenty-One:
Dream Warriors

"Rowan? How did you get in here?"

Rowan followed the voice, letting his eyes adjust to the blackness. "I came to offer you some comfort, a night of restful repose if you'll allow me." Gone was the drunken act he had put on for the guards; in its place was the cool, calculating fox here to assist the queen in her time of need.

"I do not sleep much anymore." She sounded stressed.

Rowan zeroed in on her voice. In the far corner of the cell was a small bed, if one could call it that: a slab with a few blankets. Aurora sat on top of it, her knees pulled up to her chest, her hair spilling around her. She appeared small and broken. Rowan put his front paws up on the bed. Even with his keen eyesight, it was hard to see her in the darkness, but her skin held an inner light that shone in this gloomy pit.

"I know, Your Grace, but I think I can help." His voice was calm. He heard her exhale and the blankets rustle. "Your Grace, if I may lie next to you, I believe I can quiet your mind a bit and allow you to rest." He heard her shift again.

"I do not see how."

Dream Warriors

"My gift is to help you see through trickery. If someone is preventing you from resting, I can help you. Can you trust me?"

Aurora shook her head. "There are no tricks, just karma." She turned her back on him in the dark. "Please go away, Rowan."

There was no command in her voice, so Rowan felt he had a chance. "Karma is an unforgiving mistress at times, but I do not believe her charms are at work here, Your Grace. I can prove that if you let me. You have nothing to lose. Lie down, please." He pulled the thin sheet over her shoulders.

The fight in her was gone; Aurora sank down onto the bed, mumbling incoherently. He stroked her hair until her breathing slowed and she fell asleep. Rowan gazed upon the queen, then climbed into bed and curled up next to her, his tail wrapped around her waist. His breathing fell in time with hers. They were both asleep when the dark cell lit up a sickly shade of purple and green, the source of the light a brand upon Aurora's back. The glow illuminated the cell for a moment, and then as quickly as it had begun, it shrank back into itself and once again only darkness remained.

Aurora traded one jail for another, opening her eyes upon her dreamscape. She recognized the jasmine field and immediately fell to her knees, sobbing.

Without warning, a hand brushed her hair. "Shh... do not cry. It is almost over."

Aurora raised her head, shaking. She recognized the voice without having to see to whom it belonged. "No, no, no! Why are you still here? I have done everything that has been asked of me!" She raised her eyes to see Awynn standing in front of her.

His dull eyes and trembling chin conveyed his sadness. "Not everything, Aurora."

She uprooted the purple flowers as she spoke. "I gave away my child to be raised by humans, I bound her gifts, and I saved Jarvok. In doing all of this, I have lost my kin. Jarvok hates me. I have protected everyone!"

"You saved everyone but me. You protected them the way you did not protect me, or Serena, or the hundreds of other Fae who died while you played war. Even now, while I tell you I am hunted, you still delay and make it easier for them to find me." His words echoed in the field.

She cried, "I am to be executed in but a day. You will find your rest when I meet my Oblivion."

Awynn shook his head. "You took too long. By then it will be too late for me."

As if on cue, the sky turned blood-red, and screeching was heard from above; the flowers wilted with every ear-piercing scream. Creatures loomed overhead. "They have found me!" Awynn yelled. "They will use my light to cross into the Veil and become stronger, doing the bishops' bidding. This will be on *you*, Aurora."

"But the bishops have the power. Why do they still need your essence? What can we do to stop them?" she called back as the cries from above grew closer and louder. A blade appeared next to Aurora. She picked it up. "If I end myself here in the dream realm, will that stop them?" she asked.

Awynn nodded. "You will not be a threat any longer. They will no longer need my essence. The dream will end, and they will not be able to collect my essence. However, it is your choice; I am not asking you to do this."

She put her hand on his shoulder. "I know, Awynn. I will do it for you." She raised the blade to her chest and prepared to plunge it into her heart.

"Yes, thank you," Awynn mouthed.

A voice called from across the field. "Queen Aurora, I command you to stop! Do not proceed!" The sky turned from blood-red to a calm shade of pink. The voice called to her again—and it was recognizable. She glanced around, searching for its source. The shrieking from above abruptly halted.

Awynn's face contorted. "What are you doing? Don't you want to protect me? Finish this!" he spat at her. The flowers sprang back to life and parted as Rowan leapt from the tall grass.

The champagne fox charged at Awynn, pinning him to the ground. He snarled as he climbed onto the Fae's chest. "Do not speak, or I shall rip your throat out," Rowan warned with a guttural growl.

Horrified, Aurora yelled at the Familiar to get off Awynn.

The fox did not take his eyes off the bishop as he addressed his queen. "Your Grace, drop the blade. Now!" His voice was commanding, and she did as he instructed, shock rolling over her.

Rowan called out to the sky. *"Lady Sybella, Oracle of the Court of Light, your Familiar calls. My eyes are yours, see what I see. Only the truth, no tricks. My ears are yours. Hear through the lies as I do."* The sky flashed, and the sun broke through the pink sky to shine as brightly as if it were a midsummer's day.

A pair of copper-flecked eyes with hints of rose gold appeared in the sky above them. Lady Sybella's silken voice echoed across the meadow. "You have done well, my Familiar." Aurora shook her head, confusion flooding her synapses. "Your Grace, be not afraid. We are all here to help you."

Aurora stumbled backward and fell into the flowers, unable to speak. Half the sky darkened, stars peeking out and twinkling in the atmosphere.

A husky voice called from the side of the meadow eclipsed by night. "Rowan, I am here." Holly, the black mink and Lady Zarya's Familiar, bounded through the jasmine. Her body undulated through the flowers and grass until she found a rock to stand on at the border of the night side.

"Merry meet, Holly," Rowan said. "I would give you a proper greeting, but as you can see, I am a bit indisposed." He growled at Awynn.

Holly acknowledged Aurora. "Your Grace, I am sorry to see you under such circumstances." The mink did not wait for a response; she rose on her hind legs and put her paws to the sky. The full moon appeared, bathing her in its silvery-blue light and making her black coat glow. *"Lady Zarya, Oracle of the Court of Dark, your Familiar calls. My eyes are yours; see what I see in the dark and cast light where there is none. Let our light illuminate all that hides in darkness. Nothing shall escape our sight."*

The moon split, and two silver irises appeared, a sign Lady Zarya had joined them. "Thank you, Holly. I am present. Lady Sybella, Rowan, Your Grace, shall we deal with this problem?"

Rowan sneered at Awynn. "With pleasure, my lady."

Aurora stood, finally finding her voice. "No, that is Bishop Awynn. I failed to protect him in life, and now... please!"

Lady Sybella spoke first. "Your Grace, this is not Bishop Awynn, as you will see. Please step back and let us show you."

Rowan jumped off Awynn. Awynn tried to reach for the fox, but a ray of sunshine hit the bishop, pinning him to the ground. The four dream walkers began a chant that had an immediate effect on Awynn:

"Power of light, shine bright, shine true; burn this form, reveal its truth. Let its lies now melt. Let their power be gone, dissolved away in the sun's new dawn. Let our light and dark release his game. Its hold is gone, he has no reins. So mote it be."

With each line, Awynn twisted and arched as if their words were daggers cutting into him. The third time they spoke the chant was the loudest, their voices reverberating across the landscape. The figure distorted and burst into flames, and Aurora screamed. Rowan held her back as the charred body gave one final convulsion and went limp.

Aurora dropped to her knees, weeping. Rowan stayed where he was, watching the blackened body. Then the body suddenly sat up, and Aurora jerked back, startled. The scorched figure tore and clawed at its skull, peeling the burnt flesh to reveal another form underneath—a shadow slipping off the flesh it was encased in. When it was finished peeling off the skin, a specter floated above what had been Awynn. It had no discerning features and was inky black, preventing them from seeing completely through it. Long, claw-like hands hung to the ground as it hovered.

Holly recognized it immediately. "Shadow Kat," she said in a hush voice, stepping closer. The night sky followed her, keeping her shrouded.

Rowan watched her warily. "Holly..." Caution rang out in his voice.

"It is from our domain, Rowan." Holly had no fear in her voice, only a healthy dose of respect. She stood a few feet from the creature. "May I address it, my lady?" she asked.

Lady Zarya's eyes lit up the night sky like a crackle of lightning. "Be careful, my Familiar."

Holly bowed her head and stretched herself tall. "Shadow Kat, your true form has been revealed in the dream plane. You are bound by the laws of the Shadow Realm to answer when questioned by another creature of the same realm who has foiled your ruse. I am Holly, familiar to Lady Zarya, Oracle of the Court of Dark. I am a creature of the Shadow Realm. You will answer my question, as is our law."

A shimmer passed over the Shadow Kat, and it turned to face Holly. "Ask your questions, Holly of the Shadow Realm, and I will answer them as best I can," the creature hissed. Awynn's inflection and dialect had vanished.

"How long have you been haunting the Fae known as Queen Aurora's mind?" Holly's tone resonated with authority.

The Shadow Kat glanced in Aurora's direction. "She is not my queen. Therefore, I do not know her as Queen Aurora and will not address her as such. The one known to you as Aurora I have haunted since her first taste of the one she calls Jarvok's aura."

Aurora shuffled forward. "That was months ago!" she called out.

Rowan tried to calm Aurora, rubbing his head on her hip, pressing his weight against the queen; anything to let her know she was not alone. "It will not answer you, Your Grace."

Holly directed her attention back to the Shadow Kat. "Who sent you to Aurora?"

"I do not know. I was not summoned to a keeper," the creature answered.

"A keeper?" Aurora whispered to Rowan.

Rowan seemed bothered by Shadow Kat's words. He narrowed his eyes, studying the interaction. "A keeper controls the Shadow Kat, directing them to their target."

Aurora nodded, satisfied.

Holly paced. "How did you find yourself attached to Aurora without a keeper?"

The Shadow Kat pondered the question. "I do not know. I was suddenly aware of my existence in her subconscious. My task was woven into my energy cloak." The Shadow Kat raised its arms for a moment, displaying the cloak, and dropped them. Its claws hung limply at its sides.

Holly sensed the creature was telling the truth.

Rowan, on the other hand, was not convinced. "Creature, that is not fathomable! What you are describing would require powerful dark Magick, the likes of which the realms of the Veil have not yet seen. You do not speak the truth."

The Shadow Kat directed its attention to the fox, as if aware of him for the first time. It floated over to him.

When it was within inches, Holly's voice thundered. "That is far enough, Shadow Kat."

The creature stopped as if it had hit an invisible wall, taking umbrage at Rowan's words. "I do not lie. Shadow Kats do not lie. We are not creatures of good or evil. We do not choose sides in the plebeian first realm, for we are not slaves to the flesh bags." The creature raised its claws in the direction of Aurora as it spoke. Rowan twitched his nose, and his blue eyes burned as the Shadow Kat addressed him. "You are merely pets of the flesh bags, when and if they choose to hold your leashes. They feed you scraps to get you to do their bidding and discard you back to the corners of the Shadow Realm."

Rowan's rage bubbled to the surface. He knew he could not strike the creature, but he would not be insulted. "Familiars are respected, honorable positions that only those who are worthy can hold. You do not know the meaning of the word *honor*."

Holly's voice echoed again, "Enough!" She flicked her eyes at both Rowan and the Shadow Kat. "I do not have time for this! Shadow Kat, you do not know who summoned you to act against Aurora, yet you received instructions embedded in your energy cloak. What were your orders, exactly?"

The creature responded best to her cold, authoritative tone. It faced her again. "My orders, as you call them, were to bring Aurora to her knees, to make her reject her crown, and to eliminate her by any means necessary."

Rowan, Holly, and Aurora exchanged glances.

"I gave up my child because of you. My little girl!" Aurora screamed, charging at the creature, but Rowan blocked her.

Once again, Lady Sybella interceded. "Your Grace, I know this is upsetting, but please, we do not have much time. We must use it wisely."

Aurora put her hand over her mouth, stifling the sobs.

The Shadow Kat spoke to Holly. "Ask me to elaborate, so I may address these accusations."

Holly agreed to the creature's request. "Shadow Kat, please expand on the nature of your mission and what your powers are."

The group all held their collective breath as the creature spoke. "As I said, I am neither good nor evil. I cannot make a target do anything. I am a manifestation of their darker emotions. If I am summoned by a keeper, it is usually with the intention to teach the target a lesson of introspection. I can search the target's mind for their guilt, anxieties, and fears. Armed with that information, I become a representation of those feelings—in Aurora's case, her own mistrust, grief, and fear of abandonment. I will walk in their dream plane, and the more attention the target gives me, the more I feed, until I am strong enough to enter the first realm and haunt their mind."

Aurora's eyes grew wide. "My hallucinations of Awynn," she whispered.

"Once I am thoroughly embedded in their mind, I can offer advice or influence the target's life, based upon the keeper's wishes. As for the idea I made Aurora give her child away, that is false. I did not."

Aurora could not hold her tongue any longer, "Liar! You told me to, you said it was the only way to keep her safe!" She wept as she spoke, Rowan supporting her.

"Shadow Kat, did you tell Aurora to give her child away?" Holly asked.

The figure hovered closer to Rowan and Aurora but respected the boundaries set by Holly. "I never told Aurora to give away her child. I suggested a course of action. It was her own pride, fear, and mistrust of her lover, Jarvok, that brought her to that conclusion. I merely preyed upon her pride and her guilt over her kin's death under her watch. She had many fears about not being able to protect another life. She felt she had failed too many in the past. I gave her suggestions on how to keep her child safe, based upon what was embedded in my cloak, but she had free will and she could have said no. If Aurora had trusted Jarvok and not given in to her worry about him being too impulsive, I would not have been able to take root. Her stubborn pride, insistence on doing things on her terms, and selfish need to be the savior to her kin allowed me to have a home in her subconscious."

Rowan had heard enough. "You evil demon! You tricked the queen into giving up her child, her life, and now you stand here and say it was not your fault, but hers!"

"Rowan, let the creature finish! Shadow Kat, please continue."

"A Shadow Kat cannot take root in the mind without fertile soil to grow. Aurora had much anxiety and fear toward the father of her child. She feared his temper and his emotional instability toward her kin. She never dealt with those feelings. She never mourned the loss of Awynn. She marked her body with symbols of dead Fae, constantly keeping herself in a state of grief and guilt. She felt she was the only one to carry the burden. This mixture of fear, anxiety, guilt, and pride makes a powerful fertilizer."

Holly trembled. "But you do not know who sent you?"

The creature raised its claws, making fists, then dropped them. "You keep asking me the same question. I will answer the same because it is the truth: no, I do not."

Holly bowed. "Oracles, are you satisfied?"

"We are," the voices replied from above.

"May I release him now?" Holly asked.

"Wait! Release him?" Rowan protested. "You mean, banish him?"

Holly shook her head. "He was but a tool in this. I will send him back to the Shadow Realm." She lifted her paws up.

"No, you cannot," Rowan protested, disgusted.

The Oracles replied in tandem to the familiar's displeasure. "Rowan, please hear us. Holly is correct. The creature did not commit the crime. It was the dagger. On its own, the dagger presents no danger, but in the hands of someone with malicious intent, the dagger becomes a weapon. When wielded by a Fae with the wrong intentions, the Shadow Kat was destructive. But, on its own, it would not have harmed Aurora. It should be set free."

Holly wasted no time. *"Shadow Kat, creature of the Shadow Realm, you are not needed here. You are free to fly, free to soar, you are bound to Aurora no more. Return to the Shadow Realm and never return to the Veil again. So says your Empress. So mote it be."*

The creature writhed and dropped to its knees. "Thank you, Empress Hecate, for your mercy."

The black mink folded her arms with her palms pressed together. A hole opened beneath the creature and swallowed it up.

"Empress Hecate?" Aurora whispered to Rowan.

"A long story for another time, Your Grace," he responded before giving Holly a respectful bow.

The mink walked over to Aurora, the night sky still flanking her. "I am sorry for your troubles, Queen Aurora, but the Shadow Kat was not completely incorrect in its assessment. Even knowing that you were manipulated, most of this was by your own hand. I tried to warn both you and King Jarvok. I am sorry it has come to this." Holly blinked, fighting back tears.

Aurora was too dumbstruck to argue.

"Lady Zarya, I am leaving this plane," Holly called out, turning to leave.

Rowan, however, felt there was more to say. Much more. He could not hold his tongue. "Aurora is innocent. Why are we letting her suffer? This is not our way! We know someone sent the Shadow Kat after her to cause her pain. I am in her cell right now, and the door is unlocked. I can let her go, and we can find the bastard—or three, if my hunch is correct—who did this and bring them to the light! We can get her child back and set things right!" He hoped he had misread the situation and they would all agree with him, but the objection came from an unexpected source.

Chapter Twenty-Two:
Responsibility

Chest heaving, Rowan stood in Aurora's dream, believing he had rallied the troops to fight for her freedom. He was ready to go forth into battle in real life, but a small voice doused his fire.

"No." Aurora stood tall, appearing more like a queen than he had seen in weeks. She wiped the tears from her eyes.

"What?" Rowan asked.

"I said 'no.' Both the Shadow Kat and Holly were correct. In one way or another, this was all by my own hand. Everything it said about my fears and holding on to guilt was the truth."

Holly peered over at Rowan, who was shaking his head in disbelief.

"We all have issues with our partners. You will work on it with Jarvok," he argued, gripping Aurora's hands in his paws.

Holly moved closer to the fox. "You are not listening to her, Rowan. You know that even if she tells Jarvok everything that has transpired with the Shadow Kat and the bishops' plot, Jarvok will take things to the extreme and burn the palace down. We also do not know who sent the Shadow Kat. You *think* it was the bishops, but what if you are wrong? Her child will not be safe. There are too many enemies in the Court of Light. Jarvok cannot possibly protect her from all of them. If he burns down the palace, everything they have worked for will be for naught. Aurora has exposed the schism between the old and new beliefs about the bloodlines mixing. If Jarvok goes crazy now without any proof, the kingdom would implode. She already looks unstable. Forgive me for the callous vocabulary." Holly's eyes were large and dark, carrying both empathy and logic.

"No! There must be another way!" Rowan yelled up at the sky, but there was no response or a flash of eyes from the Oracles above. "This is what we do! Why are you all willing to sit back and let Aurora die? Don't you have something to say?"

Holly looked at her longtime friend warmly. "Rowan, you know the rules. The Oracles cannot interfere in matters of death or free will."

Aurora knelt and put a hand on the fox's back, grasping his warm, soft fur. "Holly is right. You both gave me excellent advice, and I should have known Awynn would never have blamed me for his death—or anyone else's. Looking back now, it seems so clear. Perhaps I wanted to be fooled; maybe I wanted this to be over. I have been queen for longer than I can remember. In some ways, I let myself be tricked. It is a harsh reality, and I must face it: I no longer deserve to be queen. Make no mistake, this is not how I wanted it to happen, and I will not make it any easier for the bishops than I already have. My child is better off with

Responsibility

the humans than in the Court of Light, surrounded by the bishops or any other enemies I may have. She will have a life." Aurora kissed Rowan on the cheek. "Thank you for showing me the light, both of you. I am eternally grateful."

Before Rowan could say anything, the world around him dissolved, and he found himself opening his eyes back in the dark cell. Rowan untangled himself from the sleeping queen. He gazed upon her for a moment, then pulled the blankets up around her. He smoothed her hair back from her face and kissed her forehead. "You are a queen in so many ways," he whispered, leaving her cell just as dawn broke.

Out in the corridor, Riker and Finn were still snoring. Rowan took the keys from Riker's belt and locked the door behind him. He thought one last time about freeing Aurora, but he knew it was not what she wanted. He shook the thought from his head and sighed as he made his exit.

Rowan walked back up the dark corridor, but there was no skip in his step this time.

"You did well, my Familiar," Lady Sybella whispered in his head.

"Thank you, my lady, but if you do not mind, I need some time alone."

"As you wish, Rowan, but remember: sometimes the universe has bigger plans for one of its stars. Her light will shine on. The decision she has made will allow for another star to shine brighter and burn hotter in the years to come."

Rowan did not respond. He climbed the stairs with a heaviness that was not in his legs, but in his heart and soul.

Chapter Twenty-Three:
Blossoms and Tea

Holly felt the sun's warmth against her fur, letting her know it was about midmorning. Her right ear twitched as she angled toward the door and listened for the fox's tune. She was grateful Lady Zarya had given her the space she needed after last night's dream-walk. The Dark Oracle was her first Fae partnership. More often than not, Holly found her human wards to be needy and clingy. However, Lady Zarya had a much better sense of her own emotional needs and wants. She recognized Holly was not a piece of property or a pet—she was a gift from the universe, not something she was entitled to. Holly would take a moment to mourn when her time with Zarya ended. She genuinely liked the Fae Oracle and found her honesty refreshing.

Holly shook her head and yawned, her small paw covering her mouth. Her jaw cracked. "Such a human response," she mumbled. Exhaustion still lingered in her body. Dream-walking took more out of her than she cared to admit, but last night's excursion had been both physically and emotionally draining. If she was feeling it, then Rowan would need a second helping of cantaloupe tea to calm his mind.

Holly sniffed the air and smiled. Ungarra had not disappointed; the sweet aroma of the fresh melon wafted in, along with the warm scent of cinnamon honey sweet buns. The redolent bouquet made her stomach growl.

Holly scurried to the small sitting area outside her bedroom. A cart with a white cotton tablecloth was positioned by the large arched window, which was open to allow the fresh morning air to flood the room. Two small chairs were placed by the cart. A vase of fresh pink and orange Gerber daisies sat in the middle of the cart to anchor the setting. The teakettle was wrapped in hot towels to keep the water warm. Two tea bowls waited at each place setting, along with a small plate for the buns. A silver cloche was next to the daisies, with smaller cloches nearby, most likely covering fresh jams or almond butter. Pressed white napkins neatly sculpted into swans decorated each setting. "Ungarra never does anything halfway," Holly said, shaking her head in amusement and respect.

A recognizable whistle sounded down the hallway. Holly concentrated on the tune; she could tell Rowan's disposition based upon his whistle. Today, his tune was a bit flat, and Holly frowned, as this meant he had not rested after their adventure. *Most likely he had stayed up praying to Mother Luna for guidance*, Holly thought. *But if Mother Luna had ordered him to free Aurora or intervene on her behalf in some way, his tune would not be flat. It was always flat when he was tired and disappointed.*

The thought of Rowan not getting any rest after such an exhausting ritual, sitting somewhere praying all alone, made what little of the heart she had left break. Rowan was inherently good, she knew; he was the most kindhearted familiar she had ever met. He still felt too deeply for his wards. He was not jaded yet. With each mission they were sent on, she thought this would be the one to kick it out of him, and it never did. Rowan always managed to keep a spark of empathy for the humans and now the Fae. Holly worried about him; his gregarious nature was endearing, and she did not want him to lose it, but she was afraid it might eventually be his downfall. He seemed much too invested in Aurora, who was not his ward. However, Rowan was not like Holly or many of the other creatures of the Shadow Realm. He was able to become human four times a year, which helped him relate to them. Holly knew it was more than that—he had been one of them once, a long time ago.

The tap at the door brought her back to the present. She opened it to see the champagne fox sitting outside, patiently waiting for his invitation.

He smiled and sniffed the air. "Good morning, Muffin! Sleep well? Any interesting dreams? Oh, is that cantaloupe tea I smell?" Holly shook her head and stepped aside to allow him in. He licked her cheek, but she quickly wiped his display of affection away. "What? Too soon for a bit of a joke?"

"Tea and cinnamon sweet buns are set. Let's get your emotional purge out of the way." Holly rolled her eyes in response to his lame attempt at covering things up.

Rowan glanced over his shoulder as he stalked to the cart. "Some days, love, you know me too well." He surveyed the spread, and his mouth watered as he removed the largest cloche, unleashing the full scent of the warm

Blossoms and Tea

cinnamon buns. His tapered snout hovering over the glazed goodies, he inhaled deeply. "I *needed* this." With the silver tongs, Rowan delicately placed a pastry on a plate for Holly and, being a gentleman, served himself last. Holly poured the tea, sliding the sugar to him first.

While Rowan sprinkled sugar into his tea, Holly observed him. The fox's usual swagger was there, but the spark was not, indicating he was still hurting from the previous night. In true Rowan fashion, he had spent all night trying to deal with it and was here to ask her to clean it up. They had done this dance for hundreds of years. She chalked it up to Rowan never letting go of the life he had left behind when he crossed over. True, it had made him charming and loveable, but it made him broody and guilt-ridden too. He was emotionally stunted at times, and this was one of those times.

The silence between the two had gone on long enough. "Did you sleep at all?" Holly inquired, scanning him with her bottomless eyes.

Rowan set down the tea bowl. "You know the answer to that, Holly." Gone were the pet names and swagger. He seemed braced for the lecture he had heard from her a hundred times before.

"Did she respond?" Holly asked in a gentle voice, trying a new tactic.

Rowan narrowed his eyes. "Of course not. The problem of one Fae queen does not register compared to all the other pawns Mother Luna has on the board." As the words fell from his mouth, his muzzle scrunched as if he was wishing he could take them back. He had inadvertently made Holly's point for her. "Oh, bloody hell!" He folded his arms in a huff.

"Rowan, Mother Luna sent us to teach the Oracles about their growing gifts. We are here for them. Even if we thought our duty might be to help Aurora and Jarvok have a successful union, they have free will—they have chosen their paths. We exposed the Shadow Kat because someone, or something, interfered in the two courts. It was a great tool to show the Oracles what they were capable of. If our purpose was to right Aurora's wrongs, Mother Luna would have spoken to you last night or compelled the Shadow Kat to give up its keeper. The eclipse is tomorrow. We are needed for our wards. I am sure we will receive our next set of instructions when her power is on full display." Holly returned to nibbling on her pastry, her whiskers twitching.

Rowan pushed his plate away. "Do you ever tire of the games, Holly? Wondering if we are doing the right thing? Pardon the pun, but do you ever think we are just chasing our own tails?" His questioning eyes were full of pain.

For the first time, Holly wondered if he had actually lost his spark. Her shoulders slumped, and she put her breakfast down. "Are you asking me if we are lost? If in not getting a response, we are like the Fae? Abandoned by our Creator? No. We are not. Mother Luna speaks to us, perhaps not as much as we would like, but she did not turn her back on us the way their Creator did. They have not heard from Him in centuries. He has moved on to humans. I feel for the Fae. It must be very difficult for them to be replaced by simpler creatures, but each God has their own way of dealing with their creations. Mother Luna would never turn her back on her children. We may not understand her methods, but it does not mean she is not here with us." Holly's paws extended over the table, her faith and passion taking over.

Rowan cast his eyes down. "It has been so long since I have met a ruler who has not been corrupted by their own demons. I thought Aurora still had good to do for both humans and Fae. I wanted to give her that chance. I wanted to believe Mother Luna would take the Fae in, much the way she took me in. I cannot comprehend how allowing Aurora to meet her end can lead to something better, not when we have dealt with the likes of Caligula, Pope John XII, or Empress Wu Zetian. Those horrible humans strangled their own offspring, raped nuns, murdered animals, and killed innocents. We had to bring their reigns to an end, but *Aurora*? It makes no sense. How can their God believe the humans are more enlightened than the Fae and worth His time? I am questioning all of it. The Fae have been trying to teach the humans about the universal energies and nature, yet they are about to endure pain and chaos. The bishops are reminiscent of the human rulers we see all the time. Their closed-mindedness and elitist attitudes toward the Dark Court is what I see the humans display toward other religions, genders, and races. It scares me."

The mink wanted to answer him, but she was at a loss for words.

The silence between the friends hung in the air until a wind swept through the room. White flowers blew through the open window. Rowan paid no attention at first.

"Rowan, the flowers!" Holly exclaimed.

"Yes, yes, they are pretty, love," he answered robotically.

"No, you troll, look!"

A white flower sailed through the window and landed on the table. His eyes grew wide. "Is that what I think it is?"

"A moonflower!" Holly cried out.

The floor was littered with white and pink blooms resembling a full skirt, with three stamens in the center. "This is impossible," Rowan whispered. "They only bloom at night and immediately close when sunlight hits them."

"This is a sign. Mother Luna is watching us, Rowan. She heard you. She does not want you to be sad. She heard your pain and is literally showering you with affection." The two Familiars danced in the blooms that rained in from the window, laughing and giggling. Rowan lay on the floor, making "flower angels" amidst the blooms, which were now so thick that the Familiars could no longer see the carpet. Holly made a crown of flowers and skipped through the blooms.

"We must stay the course," Rowan said, resolute.

Holly smiled. "She hears us and watches us."

"We did what was asked of us last night even though it brought us pain. We did what we were supposed to do. We must trust in Mother Luna that this is all for something bigger. We freed Aurora of the Shadow Kat and taught the Oracles there is another level to their power. That is all that was asked of us, and tomorrow we will help them through the eclipse and mourn Aurora from there. We will move on if those are Mother Luna's wishes," Rowan said, and Holly nodded. As the last of the flowers settled on the floor, Rowan whispered, "Thank you."

Chapter Twenty-Four:
Heavy Is the Heart That Wears the Crown

The execution was public. Everyone from the Courts of Light and Dark were invited to attend. The Spelaions constructed a small platform overnight, ten feet across and ten feet wide. A timber pole was in the center, with rope neatly looped to the side. It seemed to be a placeholder, though, as a black crystal pole was being readied to take its place.

Illuminasqua waited at the top of the towers and along the crystal causeways. The palace guards stationed themselves along the perimeter of the platform to keep the crowd back. The royal veranda overlooked the platform. Zion paced there now, tapping the Angelite disc scar in the middle of his forehead. His stress-induced rhythm quickened as he watched Fae stream into the courtyard below. It was turning out to be a lovely summer's day. He looked upward, noticing ribbons of cinnamon, lavender, and blue coming into their own as the sun took its place in the sky. The clean smell of jasmine and rain filled his lungs, washing away the ugliness of the night. He almost felt like things were going to be all right, but he knew this was nature's illusion.

Zion glanced through the veranda's open doors. The Dark Fae King sat just out of reach of the sun's rays, wrinkling his nose at the floral aroma. Their natural remedies could not touch Jarvok or his heart, nor could their tinctures heal him; he only craved vengeance.

Asa, stoic as always, stood behind Jarvok's chair. Dragor, Yanka, Raycor, and six other dragons flew above the palace, casting their shadows on the balcony as they circled the courtyard.

Zion gestured for Asa to join him. "What is taking them so long?" His voice was laced with agitation.

"They said they would let us know when the arrangements have been made. Lady Zarya is preparing with Sybella. Yagora and Azrael are doing a sweep. Please stop pacing, Zion, you aren't easing anyone's tension," Asa said, eyeing Jarvok. Zion followed her gaze and took the hint.

Bishop Geddes entered the room. "King Jarvok, are you ready?"

At the bishop's words, Zion went to stand next to his king, Asa following him.

Jarvok stood to face the bishop, who was dressed in his all-white uniform. The king looked the bishop up and down. He had half expected the man to be dressed in black, given the circumstances.

"Where are your comrades?" Jarvok asked.

"They are busy with last-minute preparations but will join us shortly," Bishop Geddes said, wringing his fingers, his eyes darting from side-to-side.

"We must discuss a few points, King Jarvok."

"What other protocols must you deliver, bishop?"

"Quee—*Aurora* has waived her right to trial. She has confessed, and because you are the, um, victim, King Jarvok, by Fae law you may choose her punishment, which, by both courts' law, is death for conspiracy to murder a king. Due to the fact Aurora was a Virtue Angel by birth, she is to meet her Oblivion by an Elestial Blade. Have you chosen which of your lieutenants you would like to carry out the, um, punishment?" Bishop Geddes straightened his shoulders, trying to appear confident.

King Jarvok stepped toward the bishop, his boots digging into the fluorite crystal floor.

Before Jarvok could speak, Zion was by his side. "Please, my liege, I beg of you to allow me to be the one to enact your punishment. Let it be my Elestial Blade driven through the one who betrayed you. I—"

Jarvok grabbed Zion by the throat and turned to stare at him. "Stand down. I have made my choice, and it is not your blade I wish to use." He pushed his loyal lieutenant back, who coughed, gasping for air. Asa dared not go to him.

Zion regained his composure and stood at attention.

Bishop Geddes focused on the imposing figure towering over him. He swallowed as Jarvok spoke.

"I have chosen who will deliver my punishment, but it will not be any of *my* Fae." Jarvok studied Geddes' face.

"Well, I am afraid we are at an impasse, King Jarvok, for only an Elestial Blade can—" Suddenly, his eyes bulged, and he dropped his head in comprehension. Jarvok smiled. Asa gave Zion a sideways glance to see if he had figured it out, and the look of defeat lining Zion's face told her he had. She could feel his heart sink.

Bishop Geddes looked up at Jarvok. "And if she refuses?"

Jarvok gave a grim smile, teeth bared. "According to your law, she is choosing loyalty to the crown over kin. Isn't that breaking her oath? It is a punishable offense—by death, I believe? Zion will be my blade for Aurora, and I will be the blade for Captain Desdemona since I am not allowed to enact my own punishment. Believe me, bishop, I wish it could be my blade to end Aurora. I would do it... gladly." He whispered the last word an inch from the trembling bishop's face.

"Yes, King Jarvok. I will make the arrangements and give her the order of execution. In the meantime, I have shown Lady Zarya to the room where the Oracles will await the eclipse. When the execution is complete, we will meet the Oracles for their readings. Once this is done, we have your word that the Dark Fae will leave the Court of Light, and the Treaty of Bodhicitta will remain intact?" Sweat formed on Bishop Geddes' brow. His breathing picked up.

Jarvok paced for a moment, relishing the growing tension. "Yes, Bishop Geddes, we will depart from the Court of Light, and the Treaty of Bodhicitta will remain intact. We will stay on our side of the River Nimbue, but do not come to our side of the Veil. You won't like what you find. The Power Angel memorial is to be returned to me. I do not care how you do it, but that is part of my retribution for this embarrassment. Those are my Fae. I want them returned! If Dark Fae blood is ever spilled again by the Court of Light, I will return, and this time I will not play by any rules of war. My dragons will rain fire, ice, and acid down on this kingdom." Jarvok's voice was a growl.

Bishop Geddes managed to find his spine during Jarvok's speech. He straightened. "I understand, King Jarvok, but the memorial stays as insurance you will not attack us. If we give it to you, there is no reason for you not to destroy our kingdom. You may visit it anytime, but it stays here." Geddes looked him dead in the eye, and Jarvok threw the chair he had been sitting on off the balcony in anger.

Bishops Ward and Caer entered the room just as Jarvok's voice rose. "How dare you. Those are my Fae. I built that memorial with my bare hands!" Jarvok raised his hands in the air for emphasis. "It is *mine*." Zion rushed in grabbing Jarvok's arm, holding him back. Jarvok shrugged Zion off as he stepped back. Jarvok's eyes were burning with rage as he stared at the bishops.

Zion glanced at Asa. They were ready to help their king, but they didn't know how.

Geddes was the calm one—gone was the meek, scared Fae, replaced by the calculating politician. "My quee—Aurora saved it from being desecrated. You lost it for hundreds of years, and given your outburst, we cannot simply let you walk out with your word. If we were to allow you to take the memorial, you might return to...what did you say? Rain fire, ice, and acid down on our kingdom? No, King Jarvok, you can visit your memorial anytime you wish, but it remains here with us as an insurance policy. Though I do have this for you." Geddes motioned to Bishop Ward, who produced a gold box containing a crystal globe the size of a large cantaloupe. The crystal glowed, and the Power

Angel memorial appeared. Geddes smiled. "You can see the memorial anytime through the crystal."

Asa stepped forward to take it, knowing Jarvok would smash it if he got his hands on it. She bowed her head in acknowledgment to Geddes.

Jarvok bit the sides of his cheeks, stunned at the turn of events. "I am not sure when the mouse became an elephant, Geddes, but make no mistake: my memorial is not an insurance policy. You, my little mouse, have made a grave miscalculation." Caer and Ward came to stand behind Geddes, and Jarvok gave them a casual glance. "I did not realize mice were pack animals. *Hmph*. Will your pack mentality last when everything is burning around you?"

It was Bishop Ward who spoke up, his eyes narrowing. "Is that a threat, King Jarvok?"

"Oh, not at all, simply an inquiry. I would never think of being disrespectful on such a sad day. You all seem so heartbroken at your beloved queen's impending exit from this plane of existence." The three bishops shrank a bit at the king's cutting remarks. "I will leave you, as you have much to do still, like deliver my mode of execution, Bishop Geddes." Jarvok turned his back on the three bishops with a dismissive gesture. Zion and Asa followed their king out to the balcony.

Outside, the sweet aroma of jasmine caught Asa off guard. The different shades of blue in her hair shimmered in the sunlight, and Yanka screeched in recognition the minute the dragon spotted her blue-flame hair reflecting off the quartz balcony. Asa shielded her eyes and looked up to see the burgundy ice dragon bank and glide effortlessly above, trying to capture her attention. She gave Yanka a slight wave, and the dragon returned to her game of tag. Asa focused her attention on Jarvok.

She was relieved to see the steel in her king's spine return. It was a reminder that perhaps Jarvok was not as hurt by all this as she suspected, but then again, her empathic gift told her otherwise. Asa dared not push any further to see how deep his emotional wounds went. She also knew the bishops were not at all upset by Aurora's impending demise.

Jarvok waited until he heard the door close before he spoke. "Lieutenant Asa, are we alone?"

She briefly closed her eyes, then opened them, revealing the incandescent glow from her one white eye. "Yes, we are alone, my liege. It is safe to speak freely." Her voice was hushed and controlled, but with an echo. Whenever Asa used her abilities, her voice resonated like her essence was anchored to the tail of a comet.

"Good. As soon as this is done and the eclipse has taken place, we leave. Have the dragons ready. I will remain to hear the prophecy, but I want the High Council Guard to leave after her execution. Zion, you will leave with the first wave. Asa will stay with me and Lady Zarya. Once the reading is complete, we will depart. I want Obendia and Drake to stay with me too. They do not need riders; Dragor can command them should I need the dragons as backup." Jarvok acknowledged his seer. "Asa, should something happen, your job is to get Lady Zarya out. The Oracle and her prophecy stone must get back to Zion. I will provide cover with Dragor and the other dragons should it come to that. I am hoping it will not. Alert the dragons and the High Council Guard of my plans—that is an order. Go! Both of you."

Despite the dismissal, Zion did not move. "My liege, why? You should leave first—let us stay and guard the Oracle."

Jarvok placed his right hand on Zion's shoulder. "I trust you. You are my second-in-command. You must go first. This whole situation is because of me. I made the deal with Aurora. I was going to marry her. She played me. I put us at risk. Her plan was to murder me, not you. I do not know if she still has friends looking to finish the job—"

"Exactly! That is why it should be me." Zion banged on his own chest, a hollow sound coming from his armor.

Jarvok smiled and pulled the Fae closer to him until they were forehead to forehead, their Angelite scars touching. Jarvok gathered his fortitude. "I know, my friend. I know you want it to be you. Thank you. But it has to be me. I will stay and face this. I am king, and trusting her was my mistake, not yours. Some may blame me for her death. Some may feel she was justified in wanting me dead. Perhaps nothing will happen, and I am being paranoid. If I don't come back, you must rule. We know both Oracles must be together for the eclipse; we have no choice. The reading must take place here. That makes us vulnerable."

Zion nodded, defeated.

"Good." Jarvok brought his lips to Zion's scar and gently kissed the gnarled flesh. In all the time Asa had known him, she had never witnessed him behave in such an intimate fashion. "I could not have chosen a better second-in-command or asked for a better son, Lieutenant Zion of the Court of Dark."

Zion choked back a cough and grabbed his king's forearm, bowing his head. "And I could not have hoped for a better king or deserved a better father...Jarvok."

The two Fae broke their embrace; nothing was left to say between them. Zion donned his helmet, as did Asa, and they bowed to their king and went to deliver their respective messages.

Once out of earshot, Zion looked at Asa. "Don't say a word. And no. I don't want to talk about my feelings. Don't go poking around in my emotions, empath." He grumbled, his voice devoid of its usual inflections.

Asa's smile was so big, her cheeks hurt. She placed her hands up in surrender, though she wanted to give him a hug, because deep down, Asa knew what the exchange had meant to Zion. "I didn't say a word." She batted her eyes at him, attempting to look innocent, but judging by Zion's expression, she was failing miserably.

"Whatever," he said, rolling his eyes. "Go find Yagora and Azrael. I'll take Pria, Jonah, and Ezekiel. Send a message to Yanka to rally the other dragons. Drake will need to be called in. Jarvok will have communicated with Dragor by now. Tell Yanka to have them meet Dragor by the west tower so he can brief them."

Asa nodded, and the two split up, moving fast through the maze of hallways that only a few days ago were unfamiliar. Thanks to their diligence—and especially to their king's adept little reconnaissance dragon—the sharp turns and geometric designs of the Court of Light's gleaming palace no longer held the mystery they once did. *Thank you, Los*, both Fae thought as they ran through the crystal halls.

Chapter Twenty-Five:
Three Bishops, a Queen, and a Mother

Bishop Geddes checked that he and the other bishops were alone, motioning for Bishop Caer to shut the door. They all took their respective seats at the large table in what was once Queen Aurora's private meeting chamber in the west tower.

"Hand me a scroll, Bishop Ward," Geddes said, gesturing.

Ward's blond hair was carefully pulled back in the traditional long ponytail and secured by a golden thread; two gold beads indicated his rank among the bishops. The beads blended seamlessly with his locks because his gleaming hair rivaled the precious metal. It was the mark of his faction, and many of his family members carried the same trait. He handed the scroll to Geddes, who feverishly wrote something down.

Caer and Ward exchanged glances, puzzled at the other bishop's frantic penmanship.

Geddes handed Bishop Ward the scroll. "Read it," he commanded.

Bishop Caer raised his hand meekly. "Are we ever going to talk about the fact that Aurora had the Galena blade?"

Geddes rolled his shoulders. "What does it matter, Caer?"

Caer hunched into himself. "Well, it means she knew what we were planning. What if she told someone?"

"And? She obviously didn't tell Jarvok, and at this point he wouldn't believe her. We are in the clear. Stop being so dramatic." Geddes glanced at Ward. "Are you finished reading it yet?"

Ward scanned the document, and his lips curved not into a smile but an acknowledgment of amusement. Ward passed the scroll to Caer to read next; he had a similar response.

"And what makes you think she will agree to do this?" Bishop Ward asked.

"It does not matter," Bishop Geddes replied, waving a dismissive hand. "If she refuses, she is in breach of her oath and subject to death. Jarvok has already volunteered to act as her executioner. Fool! He is so blinded by his hatred for both her and Aurora. He is the one who gave me the idea." Geddes sneered.

Ward shifted in his chair uneasily. "How does this solve our problem? What if she doesn't refuse?"

Geddes smiled, though it was cold, more like a serpent. "Those who are loyal to Aurora will never forgive Desdemona. Nor will they ever follow the captain after she kills the queen. Who would ever trust the Fae who plunged her Elestial Blade into their beloved Aurora's heart?"

The other bishops mulled over his logic. "Who shall deliver the scroll with these orders to Desdemona?" Ward asked.

Geddes chuckled. "Someone who is of no consequence to Desdemona but is adored by Aurora. It will compound her guilt."

Hogal had no idea why he was given the task of delivering a scroll to Desdemona on such a sad day. He had planned to spend the time in his shop surrounded by fire and metal, the only items that brought him solace or made sense to him. When you heated gold, it melted; he could mold it and turn it into something beautiful, erase its past life, smooth away its rough edges, and voilà, it took on a new form. Add heat, break the solid form down to liquid, remold it, let it cool, and you had something new. There was no emotion to metalwork. All the variables were accounted for. An impurity in his raw material usually turned into a happy accident, making his work more spectacular. There was nothing he had not seen or overcome in his centuries of metalwork. True, there was some emotion when he sculpted, but making the gold malleable was not Magick or based on personality. It was simply a basic elemental reaction he had mastered through practice. After hundreds of years as one of the last metalworkers since Marco met his Oblivion, Hogal had learned to love the solitude of his shop and metals even more. Fae contact was rare for him. Aurora had been one of the few Fae who could get him out of the shop, and once she was gone, he might not see the light of day again. The next queen would

Three Bishops, a Queen, and a Mother

never truly be his queen, not like Aurora was. Aurora had been more than a monarch. She was his friend.

Hogal looked up to see he was at Desdemona's private quarters. He had been so lost in his own grief, he hadn't realized how fast he was walking or the distance he had covered. The captain and founder of the Illuminasqua had always scared him. He took a deep breath and knocked on her door, glancing around nervously as he waited. The door slowly opened to reveal the captain dressed for the afternoon's events, her all-black garb accented by the liquid midnight cape she only wore during formal rituals.

"Yes, metal Gnome, what can I do for you?" Her voice was devoid of all warmth, much like an empty grave.

"Mes been told to give this to you." He handed her the scroll.

She gestured for him to step inside her room, which was plain. It contained the bare essentials: a neatly made bed, a desk with parchment stacked in the center, and a bookcase stuffed with books. Hogal had a hard time reading the titles that occupied the shelves. On the wall to the left of the door hung weapons that glinted in the light. He was sure there was a strategic reason for their placement. However, what caught his eye was a full-sized dress form with a beautiful pale-blue and silver brocade gown adorned with folded metal wings. The arc of the wings started just above the shoulders of the form, and the wingtips grazed the floor. Hogal stepped closer. He knew his own work when he saw it. He remembered Aurora asking him to make the body form and the wings, but she never told him who or what it was for. He glanced at Desdemona but said nothing.

She looked down, not ashamed, but not thrilled the cat was out of the bag. "It is my exaltation gown," she said. "I was stripped of my Kyanite armor and given a gown to wear as a full Virtue. I received it when I was presented to Earth as the Virtues' guard. Aurora was the only one who showed up and met me. Back then she was known as Xi. Once I came to Earth, Aurora... she knew I hated it, and she allowed me to wear whatever I wanted. She saved my gown so I would never forget I was the only Power to ever exalt. Aurora presented it to me the day the palace was finished, and my quarters were done. It was a generous and thoughtful gift. I should have known she had you make the form and wings, Hogal. I never said thank you, so, thank you." She smiled at Hogal, who tried to smile back.

"What's sayin' on the scroll?"

As she broke the wax seal, Desdemona shook her head as if trying to clear the memories. "It's from the bishops. Oh, joy." Her eyes scanned the scroll, her face at first unreadable, but as she read, her face gradually betrayed her. Without warning, her Elestial Blade impaled the scroll and incinerated it. She let out a scream of rage, feeling as though her heart was being shredded.

Chapter Twenty-Six:
Opportunity Knocks

As they waited to hear Desdemona's response to their orders, Geddes paced. He was pleased the two Fae lines would not mix and that their bloodline would remain pure. But the next issue to tackle was picking a new monarch since they alone held the power of succession. "Aurora did not have an heir, or at least not one worthy enough." Geddes struck his finger in the air. "We can only select from the heads of houses."

Ward jumped in with his two cents. "We will require someone who shares our views on the Court of Dark. Someone who is willing to strengthen our power base with the human monarchies in Europe and let the Vatican know of our true angelic nature."

Geddes nodded in agreement. "I prefer to announce the new monarch before her execution and try to convince Aurora to cooperate. Her endorsement would help repair the fracture that occurred because of her horrific choice to marry Jarvok and unite the Courts."

Ward tapped his staff on the floor. "Some factions had felt it was time to bring the two lines together, while others went along with her simply because she was queen. But there were many Fae who supported us in our beliefs that the two bloodlines should never mix."

Geddes stopped pacing and banged his staff on the floor, louder than Ward had. "The Court of Light is derived from the mighty Virtue Angels, only second to Archangels in the hierarchy. The Power Angels were lowly, beneath us. When Aurora decided to turn the tables on us and got caught trying to kill Jarvok, several Fae saw her as a martyr to their cause. No one knew she was trying to protect her dirty little secret. We must pray Jarvok never finds out she was pregnant." He threw his hands up, his cape billowing.

They still did not understand her end game. All they could do was thank the universe that Jarvok's ego was blinding him to what was unfolding right in front of his eyes. However, they also knew Jarvok was not to be underestimated. The faster they killed Aurora and rid themselves of the Dark Fae, the sooner things could return to normal in the Court of Light. So far, they had Aurora on lockdown, keeping away all visitors. As far they knew, no one else was aware of the abomination; while their source had told them of a letter, it had been destroyed in Jarvok's rage and paranoia.

Caer raised his hand timidly. "Bishop Geddes, we still have the Oracle reading to contend with. What if they see our involvement and tell Jarvok?"

Geddes whipped his head around like a viper ready to strike. "I plan on keeping the Court of Dark away from the prophecy readings after the execution. We will kill Zarya if the Dark Fae's Oracle speaks of the child, and deal with the consequences afterward."

Ward arched an eyebrow at Geddes. "While I don't have an issue killing the Dark Fae's Oracle, if we kill Zarya, Lady Sybella will meet her Oblivion. You do understand that, Geddes? It could put the Court of Light at a disadvantage. We will be without an Oracle for years, and Wendoura passed on, so there is no Fae to train a new one either."

Geddes made a dismissive gesture. "Another set of Oracles will be born to take their places. They are disposable." He stroked his goatee. "Wendoura's passing, however, poses an issue. Search the Azurite and Sphaeram Factions to see if any Fae has come close to her skills, perhaps a descendant."

Caer bobbed his head, though whether he was agreeing with the other bishop's plans or just going along, he did not say.

Geddes continued barking orders. "We will keep everyone away from the readings, making sure we are the only ones there to control the flow of information. The last and most important piece is to name Aurora's successor. Crisis averted, my bishops." He clapped his hands with an air of vindication and victory.

Caer pulled at his eyebrow.

There was a knock at the door.

Chapter Twenty-Seven:
It's Just My Heart That Hurts

Desdemona forgot she had company until the Gnome's calloused hand touched her shoulder. She could feel the pressure of his hand through her cape. She didn't realize she'd sunk to her knees or stopped screaming and started to cry.

Hogal said nothing, his wiry white eyebrows scrunched up. Desdemona pulled herself together, ashamed of her reaction. She stood up and wiped her eyes. "I have been given Aurora's order of execution." Her voice held no emotion, shock taking root in her heart. Hogal stepped away from her, hands at his mouth. The silence spread between them.

It took him a few minutes, but he finally found his words. "No, yous can't, yous ain't serious?" Hogal ran forward and pounded on her thighs, which was as high as he could reach. His eyes filled with tears. "No, yous wouldn't, hows?"

Desdemona did not fight back. She stood unmoving like a crystal pillar, taking her punishment from the Gnome.

Hogal finally tired himself out and collapsed to the floor, still crying. "No, no, pleases," he mumbled.

Desdemona lifted the Gnome to his feet and repeated the words of her oath in a soft whisper, trying not to let herself break again. "Loyalty to kin, not to the crown."

Hogal buried his head in his large hands. His bristly hair stuck out, his sobs becoming louder. "I wills never ... forgive yous ... if yous do this," he managed in between hiccups.

"I would not expect you to. I will not be able to forgive myself."

"Then dons't do its." He looked up at her, pleading.

"If I don't, I am breaking my oath and will be put to death. The bishops will have won. No one will be left to stand for the good of the kin or for Aurora's sacrifice. She will have died in vain. If I live, I can carry on her message." Desdemona wasn't sure if she was trying to convince him or herself.

"Theys won'ts lets me says my goodbye. Nots evens one goodbye I gets. She's alls I haves. Mes goings to be alones now. I didn't get one last hug, just one hug. Mes always acted like mes hated them but hers hugs felt like home." Hogal pointed skyward.

Desdemona knew what he meant, and her heart ached for him. She tried to swallow past the growing tightness in her throat. "You will never be alone again, Hogal. I am here for you." She bent down, holding his wrists. "I know we may have had our differences, but you and I are a lot alike."

Hogal shot her a disparaging glare and yanked his hands away.

She tightened her mouth but gave him space. "No, really, we are. Aurora took us both in when no one believed in us or thought we were misfits. She reminded us there was more to us than meets the eye. We need to do that for each other now. I am not very good at this touchy-feely stuff, but I will try, if you will." Desdemona extended her hand.

The metal Gnome took his red beanie off and stared at her hand. "Mes appreciate the offer and mes will try, but how can mes when yous about to kills her?"

And there it was, the ugly truth. Desdemona's heart broke all over again. She knew why she had to do it, but that didn't mean it would hurt any less. The Gnome and the warrior Fae were at an impasse, each one wanting to move forward but too scared of what it meant. They stood frozen by their own emotions, the afternoon light bathing them in a soft, warm glow. Hogal was losing the only friend who treated him like the true artist he was, who respected him for his skills, and the joy he found in giving things new purpose. He loved creating beauty, but his small, calloused appearance caused him to be dismissed and overlooked by nearly everyone he met. Aurora had always seen his beauty and light. She saw past the salty attitude and gave him love. She enjoyed listening to him talk about his work and how he would transform the ordinary into the extraordinary. He would miss their talks and the way she kissed him on the forehead. He would miss when she said, "All my love and light."

Aurora had taught Desdemona to embrace her power and never apologize for doing her job better than anyone else. She taught her hat honor and respect made a warrior, not the number of kills. Aurora had encouraged Desdemona to be proud of her background as a Power Angel, while others saw it as something to be ashamed of. Aurora respected Desdemona's cunning and prowess, but she had wanted her to learn she was more than her job. Aurora had believed Desdemona was also the only one capable of protecting the Fae, which was why she had made her take the oath of loyalty to the kin, not the crown. After centuries, Desdemona finally understood. She would not let Aurora down.

Desdemona took Hogal's hands again, which dwarfed her own, and this time he did not pull away. "You may never forgive me, and I understand, but from this day forward I will always protect you, Hogal. While I live and breathe, you will never fear anyone." She kissed the Gnome on the forehead, then walked toward the door.

"Desdemona?"

She glanced over her shoulder. "Yes?"

He took a deep breath, as if he was gathering all his strength. "Tell her... all mes love and light, please?" His eyes brimmed with unshed tears; if he blinked, it would cause a waterfall.

Desdemona turned back toward the hallway, afraid she couldn't control her emotions much longer. Her right hand balled into a fist around the door handle and her knuckles turned white. "Of course, Hogal. Stay in my room if you'd like or stay in your shop today. I will check on you tomorrow."

Desdemona closed the door and made her way toward what lay ahead: her oath, her queen, and the end of their time together.

Chapter Twenty-Eight:
It's Not Nice to Upset Mother Nature

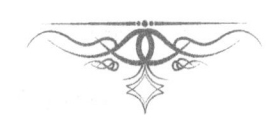

The knock at the door made the bishops go still. If it was Desdemona, she would not have bothered to knock; surely, she would have barreled through the door and impaled them with her Elestial Blade.

"Announce yourself!" Bishop Caer exclaimed. He shrugged at the others as if to say *did you have a better suggestion?*

Long green vines snaked through the crevices around the door. The vines felt the door handles like the hands of someone fumbling in the dark. They pressed the latch, and the door unlocked. The bishops watched the vines retreat from whence they came. Finally, the doors opened to reveal a tall, dark-skinned man whose mahogany complexion appeared to be infused with gold dust. He had prominent cheekbones and amber-colored eyes framed by ivy leaf eyebrows.

It's Not Nice to Upset Mother Nature

The warrior stood at attention. His green-tinged hair was cut very short, his scalp visible underneath. His muscular body was honed to athletic perfection and draped in a uniform of gold leaf–embossed body armor. Gold gauntlets with a tree insignia covered his forearms. A woman in similar dress stood beside him, his mirror image.

Orion stepped forward and greeted the bishops. "I present Lady Sekhmet, Head of the House of Hathor." The same vines that had opened the door crept back in, flooding the room with blossoming flowers as a voluptuous figure sashayed into the doorway. Her long blond, pastel-streaked hair was draped in wildflowers of every color. Her complexion changed in the light from porcelain white, to the shimmering sands of the desert, to the bark of her beloved sequoia. As Mother Nature she enjoyed wearing the colors of all her creatures.

Lady Sekhmet was beautiful. Her eyes were the color of the sky on a summer's day, her lips the red of a perfect rose. Her cheeks held the faintest blush of pink spring tulips. Her physique was that of a woman who enjoyed life. She had curves in perfect proportion to her height. Her long white empire waist gown trailed behind her, and the vines seemed to appear under her feet with each step. For a moment, Bishop Ward struggled to pay attention because he thought he could hear bluebirds singing.

As she stepped closer to the bishops, they could see her hair was like a rainbow after a sun shower, pale: almost white-blond, with pastel streaks of the color spectrum woven throughout it. They had never seen her so radiant.

She turned to her guards. "Leave us. See we are not disturbed." Even her command was melodic. When Orion and Ora exited, she gestured for the bishops to sit. "Well, let's get down to business, shall we?"

The bishops stared dumbfounded at their visitor, who in their opinion was taking an awful lot of liberties. "While it is lovely to see you, Lady Sekhmet, we are very busy," Bishop Geddes said, trying to be polite. The group sat cautiously.

"Naming Aurora's successor? Yes, it is why I am here," she replied in a matter-of-fact tone.

The bishops exchanged glances. "I am afraid we do not understand," Bishop Geddes said.

"It is simple. I am Aurora's successor." She put her hands on her hips. The bishops laughed, more uncomfortable than amused, and Lady Sekhmet joined them for a moment in their chuckles. The bishops did not notice the ivy vines winding up their chairs until it was too late. They were yanked back against their seats and secured there.

"Now that I have your attention, we can speak. I am sorry to go about it this way, but you insulted me by laughing." Her voice still had its lilt, but her eyes looked more like storm clouds than a clear blue sky.

"What is the meaning of this?" Bishop Ward demanded.

"Shut up and listen. You will name me Aurora's successor. You need a monarch who can fix this mess. A ruler who is strong, who can keep the Court of Light in line and bridge the gap that Aurora's delusion has created." With a wave of her hand, the ivy vines dropped.

The bishops leaped up, brushing the remnants of leaves off their uniforms. "Why would we choose you after that display of... of..." Bishop Caer searched for his words.

"Power?" Lady Sekhmet said, standing tall. "I needed to show you I am not afraid of anything, and I don't just

It's Not Nice to Upset Mother Nature

make flowers bloom. I am as powerful as Aurora. I am Mother Nature." As she spoke, the vines encompassed the entire room. "I control life! My guards rival the Royal Guard of the Court of Light. Combine them with the Illuminasqua, and we would be unstoppable. I am worshiped by the humans. I can restore the Court of Light to its former glory." She folded her hands in front of her, and her eyes returned to their perfect sky blue.

"We can select who we want, Sekhmet. We don't need you." Bishop Caer's tone was defiant.

Lady Sekhmet smiled, stalking over to him. "The court is fractured. You have a large secret you are trying to hide. Many do not trust you because you have sealed their beloved queen's fate. It appears you are siding with the Dark Fae. Aurora will not cooperate with you. She will never support who you name as her successor."

Bishop Caer shot his fellow bishops a look for help.

"And who told you such lies?" Bishop Ward spat.

"I have eyes and ears everywhere." A small vine crawled up her leg and cuddled her shoulder. She rubbed her cheek as the vines gathered to cradle her back. "Nothing escapes my knowing."

The bishops shifted uncomfortably. "What are you offering us?" Geddes finally asked.

Sekhmet's eyes sparkled. "I knew you were the brains behind the Galena blade switch. I will get Aurora to name me as her successor."

"But how?" Geddes' voice shot up an octave, betraying his disbelief.

"Leave her to me. When I do get her support, you will have no choice but to name me as queen. I will work with you bishops, not against you. In return, you will advance the House of Hathor to prominent status. Orion and Ora will take their place with Desdemona in the Royal Guard. You will see to it that the Illuminasqua and my guards are blended into one force. They will learn Synchron. I will produce an heir from the House of Hathor, securing my place and my faction as Fae royalty forever. Do we have an understanding?"

The bishops looked at each other and back to Lady Sekhmet. "May we have a minute to discuss your generous offer?" Bishop Geddes inquired.

"Oh, but of course. I shall step outside onto the veranda." Before walking through the rose quartz archway, she stopped and gave them a sly look. "Oh, and bishops? Remember: it isn't kind to try and fool Mother Nature."

Chapter Twenty-Nine:
No Place for Little Ones

"Orderly lines, no pushing," a member of the Royal Guard called out as the swarm of Fae filtered through the Hematite Gate. Fae from every faction were gathering, prey and predators walking shoulder to shoulder. Even the Oberons and Selkies entered the Court of Light's courtyard together. The dwindling numbers of the Aubane Factions' white deer were almost swallowed up in the sea of Fae funneling through the courtyard. Cloaks of every color denoting a Fae's social status could be seen, making the crowd look like a carnival rather than a funeral march. Yellow silk banners with Aurora's Sylph sigil rippled in the air in support of the queen, carried by a few brave Fae, while others held effigies of Aurora with knives stuck into the heart. They all gathered around the platform, it acted as a magnet for the mob, the circle closing in. This newly erected edifice holding their attention was the star of the day's event. The stage upon which a tragedy or triumph of a queen would play out, some approached gleefully, while others could hardly look.

As more Fae squeezed into the courtyard, movement grew increasingly difficult. Then the chanting began. "Kill her" and "Long live the queen" fought for dominance in the crowd, with the cries becoming louder and more emboldened. The shoving made the crowd look like a wave crashing upon a sea wall as they surged toward the platform.

"I said no shoving!" a guard yelled from atop the platform. He aimed his bow toward the mass of Fae. They quieted down for a few minutes, but the banners and effigies lurched up and down with just as much fervor as before.

"This is no place for the Little Ones," one Fae woman told her friend. The crowd shoved them forward into the courtyard, and the younger woman tightened her grip on a little Fae boy's hand. He mouthed "ow, ow, ow" to no one as the trio were jostled. The Fae boy pulled away from the two—his cousin Dora and his mother—and stared at the reflecting pools, the water eerily still. The creatures that swam beneath the blue water often lounged on top of the large pink and white lotus flowers, but not today.

When the crowd finally came to an abrupt halt, the little Fae ran into the trunk of a tree, or at least he thought that was what it was. He looked up to see it was not a tree, but a Dryad. He stared, mouth agape.

"E! Pay attention. Watch where you're walking," his cousin spat. She always called him E, everyone did. But E hardly heard her, staring in wide-eyed wonder. It was rare to see a Dryad outside their forest. It was supposedly unhealthy for them to uproot themselves, and his mother had said they were cranky when away from their soil. The small Fae shrank backward as the tree-like woman found her place among the crowd, undeterred by the run-in.

E scanned his surroundings: Apollines, Will-o-Wisps, Pixies, and the Aubane and Selkie Factions were scattered about. The heads of houses could be seen on the balconies above them. He had to put his hands up over his eyes to shield against the sun, but he could very easily spot Lady Danaus, Head of the smaller Papilionem House. She was dressed in a long, bright-green gown with butterflies that sparkled when the sun hit it just right. Everywhere Lady Danaus went, her butterflies followed. She was their guardian.

Lady Danaus' Viceroy Faction had fought alongside E's father in the Fae war. He liked Lady Danaus. She was always sweet to him when she and her mate would come to meet with his father. But that was before the war—she never smiled anymore. Many of the Fae children thought she was mean, but E knew better. His father had told him Lady Danaus had lost her love in the war, and her butterflies floated around her, trying to make her smile again. Lady Danaus was one of the few heads of houses with short hair. Many Fae kept their hair on the longer side, because as Angels, everything was dictated for them, including their hairstyle. After Lady Danaus' mate died fighting in the war, she cut her hair. Her mate had liked her hair long and flowing, and it was a painful reminder of the loss. E felt how sad and lonely she was, but he liked that she had her butterflies to keep her company.

E's attention shifted from Lady Danaus when he noticed her pointing to the platform at the end of the reflecting pools. The platform was held up off the ground by four stone posts. There was one set of stairs on the left, only wide enough for one person to go up or down. In the center of the platform was a black crystal post. E held his hand out to sense what type of crystal it was, closing his eyes to concentrate. "Black onyx," he whispered to himself.

This time it was his mother's voice distracting him. "I don't understand why this has to be public. She was, I mean, *is* a good queen. She deserves better." Her voice hitched, and she brought her hands to her face.

Dora embraced her aunt. "I know, auntie, but we must be strong. The bishops are going to crown the next queen. We cannot be seen as rebels. Uncle would not have wanted that."

E glanced between the two of them, feeling their sadness wash over him. "Can I go play? Pleeaaase?"

Dora rolled her eyes, her green hood falling off her head. "Fine, E. Go. Stay out of trouble and where we can see you!" Her voice was stern.

E waved goodbye as he pushed his way through the crowd. Fae shouted, making their points about Aurora to anyone who would listen. Some waved a banner or fist, and many cried, dreading what was to come. A few just stood quietly, their eyes unfocused as the world went by them.

There was plenty for E to watch—in his small village, most of the factions looked alike. His only experience with different Fae, besides Lady Danaus, was when Queen Aurora would come to visit his village. She would show the children her energy wings. Theadova usually escorted her too. E liked Queen Aurora the best of all the other Fae. She shook his hand when they met and spoke to him not like a child but not like a grownup either. He couldn't put it into words. E had a way of knowing when someone was truly good; it didn't matter if they said polite things or acted nicely, he could see their colors. His momma had told him it was the same gift his grandmother Wendoura had. His grandmother was from the Sphaeram Faction, but she was also a dual elemental and was part Azurite too. E liked his ability but found it difficult when people's colors didn't match their words. E would have to act politely anyway, which he hated doing because then his own colors wouldn't match. When E's colors didn't match his actions, he felt nauseous.

E was balancing on the edge of the reflecting pool when he heard his name called. He didn't have to search the crowd—he knew who it was. Before he could reply, a blond girl skimmed over the water and used the lily pad to bounce onto a gigantic goldfish that had picked the wrong time to pop up out of the water. She used its head as a springboard and land daintily in front of her best friend.

"Hey, E! I am so happy I found you!" the little Fae said with an infectious smile. This was his best friend, Indiga. She was a Caelam Fae or Wind Rider. Indiga was connected to the element of Air, and her eyes matched the sky on the bluest day you could imagine.

"So, you got stuck coming too?" E asked. He splashed at the water with his foot.

"Well, with my uncle and all, of course I had to come." She pointed toward the palace.

"Oh, right." E felt bad he had said anything. Indiga's parents had been killed, and she was a ward of the palace.

"Wanna play hide and seek?" Her long golden hair danced around her, caught up in the breeze that always followed her.

"Well…" E rubbed the side of his face in contemplation. He was supposed to stay close to his mother and cousin, but when he glanced over toward his mother, he noticed her wiping her eyes. He didn't want to watch while she cried.

Indiga gave him her best pout. "Oh come on. We won't go far," she wheedled. "I'm soooo bored, E," she added with a bit of a whine.

"Okay, but we have to stay close by," he said, still not sure it was a good idea.

"Great! Close your eyes and count." She squealed and her eyes lit up to an even brighter blue, which E knew was never a good sign. He exhaled slowly, already regretting saying yes.

E closed his eyes and began counting. "No flying, Indiga, that's cheating!" he called out, but when she didn't respond, he opened his eyes to see her hair bopping away toward the palace. "Oh no, you don't! I said to stay close, Indiga!" He looked back at his mother and cousin, and then to Indiga, who gave him a mischievous grin before she disappeared through the corridor toward the palace.

E rolled his eyes and chased after her. *I am totally going to get in trouble today. I know it.*

Chapter Thirty:
An Empath's Work

Asa found Yagora and Azrael with the Oracles. The four Fae were gathered in a room dubbed the Contemplation Room. Aurora had commissioned it for human visitors who were there to ask for the Court of Light's assistance.

Asa was astounded at the depth of thought and insight that had gone into the planning of such a space. The crystals Aurora had chosen in its construction were used to help calm and center the mind and spirit. This was to help the visitor to home in on what they truly needed to ask for, and to communicate it to the queen. For that reason, the Oracles felt the Contemplation Room would be the best place for their prophecy reading.

Yagora and Azrael had conducted a security sweep of the room, looking for ward charms that could potentially block either Oracle's sight. They had also secured the windows so that no one could endanger or disturb the Oracles or the members of either court during the reading. Only the leaders of both courts and their most trusted advisors could be present during an Oracle prophecy reading. Both Oracles must hold hands during the ritual, and they would speak and transcribe what was said onto the prophecy stones for posterity. Only when they joined hands could both courts hear the prophecies. Once separated, the Oracles would not remember the other's prophecy. It was a small window of opportunity, which was why it was so important to be present for their readings.

The readings done during the summer and winter solstices were considered lesser readings, usually about fertility, human political relations, and natural disasters. Eclipses, such as the one that would occur today, resulted in universe-shifting readings. These were exceedingly rare and often came with life-altering messages.

Today, Sybella and Zarya were dressed in plain cloaks, Zarya in silver, representing the moon, and Sybella in gold, representing the sun. The solar eclipse meant Zarya would receive her message first, as the moon would eclipse the sun. Her pale moonstone was placed on a makeshift altar alongside Sybella's bright sun stone. Their prophecies would be transcribed onto the stones as they spoke. Under normal circumstances, this reading would take place on neutral ground at the Archway of Apala, but nothing about today was normal.

Asa gave Yagora and Azrael a look and gestured toward the door. "King Jarvok is waiting for you at the royal veranda." The two Fae surveyed the room one last time and made their way out, as instructed.

"Lady Zarya, we will see you afterward," Asa said, turning to leave.

Lady Sybella caught the blue-haired Fae by the arm. "Lieutenant Asa, may I have a word, please?"

Asa tried to hide her surprise at the Oracle's request. "What is it, Lady Sybella?" They had no business to discuss, but because she was an Oracle, Asa was polite. She removed her helmet out of respect, indicating she was open to the conversation, though her mask stayed in place.

"You have empathic abilities, do you not?"

Asa narrowed her eyes at the bronze-skinned beauty. "What of my abilities, Lady Sybella? You know what I can do."

Sybella cocked her head as if examining the other Fae's response from every angle. "Have you seen Queen Aurora?" She pointed at Asa.

Asa was beginning to grow bored with what she considered a nonsensical line of questioning. "Get on with it, Oracle."

Sybella put her hands down, shoulders slumped. "I am sorry if I have offended you."

Asa shook her head. Oracles were considered neutral. She knew she needed to be more patient with Lady Sybella. "No, I should be the one to apologize, my lady. The bishops have your que—I mean, Aurora, on lockdown. No one has seen her. I am surprised you do not know this or have not been afforded a visit to take her last words."

Sybella glanced at Zarya, who gave a slow, deliberate nod to her antithesis. "No, I have been denied all access to my queen. However, it is neither here nor there. Asa, has anyone ever explained what exactly the rules of our gifts are?"

Asa took a dramatic breath, unsure where this conversation was going. A small click of the door indicated the two Fae were now alone; Zarya, too, had left. "Speak freely, please, Lady Sybella. I must get back to my king."

The Oracle nodded. "As Oracles we have the gift of sight, but we cannot interfere with free will or the order of the universe. If someone is meant to fall from a ledge because their fall will cause a wall to be built, saving hundreds of others, we must let them fall. Our gifts have limitations as well. One must ask us for our advice. We cannot dole it out without the correct question being posed. We can read intentions and some motivations. However, you as an empath can tap directly into someone's emotions and read their true intentions at that very moment. You know a person's deepest secrets, and they do not have to write a contract or treaty; you can reach out and feel their aura. No permission must be granted. That must be a marvelous gift. To see intention versus motivation…the fire of the soul versus their ego of motivation. To know the why of the soul. It is so profound." Sybella ran her fingertips over the back of the armchair separating them, glancing up at Asa.

"That is not exactly how my gift works. It is limited as well, and I don't go barging into people's auras," Asa said, more nervous about this topic of conversation than annoyed.

"Didn't you question why you didn't feel Aurora's oncoming betrayal of Jarvok? I am sure you only felt respect and affection emanating from her."

Asa tried to recall if she had read anything from Aurora that day that was out of sorts. The Oracle had a point. She would have sensed this murder plot. Perhaps that was what had been gnawing at her since Aurora had been caught—it was out of character for Aurora—but Jarvok had always taught her not to trust a Virtue. Perhaps Aurora had found a way to shield her deception. "My king did not ask me to read her. I do not go where I am not asked."

An Empath's Work

The Oracle paced. "Since her confession, you haven't been curious, just a bit?" Sybella made a graceful motion with her thumb and index fingers, leaving just a little space between her fingers and squinting.

Asa ignored the question. "My king is waiting for me. I must go. I am sure you have much to do to prepare for the eclipse." Asa donned her helmet and abruptly took her leave.

Sybella bowed and watched the petite, armor-clad figure disappear. Asa was formidable and gifted, but it was contained in such a compact package. Under the hard armor she still had much untapped potential. *If she only knew, she would not restrict her abilities with those trinkets...*

Sybella shook her head with pursed lips.

Once outside the Contemplation Room, Asa stood against the wall for a moment, catching her breath. She hadn't realized she had been holding it. The Oracle's words rang in her head: "intention versus motivation... the fire of the soul versus their ego. To know the why of the soul..."

Asa shook her head. They were Angels; they had no soul. She read emotions. She was an empath. She could sense another Fae's emotion—their emotionality in that moment—and from there deduce what they might do. She could not predict the future like the Oracles. If Aurora was going to try to kill Jarvok, there was no way Asa would have known. Was that what the Oracle had been insinuating?

No, this was not my fault. Jarvok had used Asa to figure out where there were ambushes or who the weakest link was in a fight, but that was all. Asa didn't know what Sybella had been trying to do, but whatever it was, she had not succeeded. The lieutenant knew she had to get her head back in the game and return to Jarvok's side.

Chapter Thirty-One:
A Friend in Need Is a Friend Indeed

The sun's rays penetrated the extremely small window of Aurora's cell. She had commissioned these cells when the war started. They were made of black Tibetan quartz and black onyx to contain Magick and prevent the captive from performing any ill-intentioned Magick. The bars were made of smoky quartz to transmute negative energy, ground it, and send it back to the earth. There was also a salt ring buried around the cell, so it could not be broken. This would keep any Magick inside the cell with the spellcaster, while the crystals worked to disperse the energy.

Aurora lifted her hand and felt the sun's weak light, its warmth a welcome comfort. She watched the shapes and forms her hand made when she broke the stream of golden light. She knew it was the last time she would see this small miracle of light and dark, shadow and illumination, and yet, she smiled at the thought. Her time was close—somewhere deep down she could feel it, the finality of it all. What irony, she thought, that her last observation would be the juxtaposition of light and dark. "You were always good for that," she whispered, directing her words to Him—the same Him she had denounced all those centuries ago on the mountaintop. Now here she was, looking to Him for refuge in her final hours, but she knew there was none to be found. He had stopped listening a long time ago. The last sound He had heard was her angelic feather falling from the mountain right after she vowed He was no longer her Father. Yes, He had heard that, so why would He be listening now? Unless He wanted to hear her tears as they hit the floor of her cell. Perhaps He would—maybe she deserved this, and He wanted a front-row seat to her day of reckoning. She dropped her hand from the sunlight and hung her head.

Aurora cried for things in the past and what was yet to come that she would never see, namely, her child. She knew it was a baby girl, but that was all she knew. She had thought what she was doing was correct, but now, sitting alone in her dim cell wondering if her little girl would ever feel sunlight dance across her face? The image broke her heart. However, she knew she could not let the bishops kill her and frame Jarvok. She had acted impulsively, but that was why she had confessed everything in the letter to Jarvok. Once he read the letter and realized they had a child, she hoped he would find the baby and take the kingdom back, even if it was too late for her. Jarvok was a good Fae. She was confident that once he had enough time to process this, he would make the choice to raise their child, unite the courts, and bring balance to the kingdoms. Their child is, after all, the first blend of the two bloodlines.

A Friend in Need Is a Friend Indeed

And if their child had a child... The idea brought a smile to her face: the two courts would be inextricably bonded forever, two parts of the same whole. A new Fae lineage.

She needed to accept her fate and believe in Jarvok. She couldn't even remember now why she had been so scared. The images of Awynn were distorted. *The Shadow Kat, damn him, but he—it, whatever it was—had made the illogical seem logical.* Aurora realized the creature had been Dragor in her dreamscape too. It had used her guilt over the Battle of Secor Valley, and her fear of the Draconians seeking revenge for the murder of their unborn. Perhaps it had even used the fact that she felt a twinge of jealousy toward Dragor because Jarvok had such loyalty from the Draconian faction. Conversely, she had bishops plotting her demise. She shook her head, knowing she should have trusted Jarvok the way she trusted him now. Aurora grabbed her head, and a silent scream escaped her.

Just as Aurora regained some semblance of herself, a voice whispered to her from the darkness in the hall, "Your Grace?" It was a woman's voice, one she recognized. Aurora scrambled to the door, listening for it again. "Your Grace? It is I, Sekhmet."

Aurora lifted her head in hope at hearing her friend's name. "Sekhmet? I am here in the last cell." She kept her voice low, so as not to alert the guards. Aurora heard footsteps growing closer to the heavy, black onyx door. There was a pause, and for a moment Aurora's heart was in her throat, her pulse drumming in her ears. Then Lady Sekhmet's face appeared like that ray of sunshine earlier, warm and inviting beyond the small bars.

"Oh, Your Grace! Thank the universe!" Sekhmet put her hands through the door to greet her queen.

"Sekhmet, how did you manage to get down here?" Aurora was happy for the company but concerned for her friend's safety. Surely, she wasn't allowed down here.

"My queen, I had to see you, regardless of the risk."

"Please, you must go. I won't allow you to risk your life for me."

"I bribed a few guards who are loyal to you, but I don't have much time. I will not abandon you in your time of need. You would not discard me if the roles were reversed," Sekhmet said in her matter-of-fact tone. Aurora hung her head, overcome by Sekhmet's display of loyalty. "My queen, what have I done wrong?"

"Nothing, but I do not deserve such loyalty. You humble me."

Sekhmet clasped Aurora's hands tighter. "Yes, you do! You are a righteous queen. I will not let you speak nonsense. You are kind and trusting. I... *we* are honored to have you. No one will ever take your place. I will certainly not pledge my loyalty to whomever those three buffoons pick next. They will not hold a candle to you."

Aurora squeezed her friend's hands. "The bishops have asked for my cooperation and support in choosing my successor."

Sekhmet scoffed. "How dare they! Well, I hope you told them no!" she said with vehemence, but before Aurora could elaborate, Sekhmet let go of one of her hands and passed a small pouch through the bars. It was a light-pink silk drawstring pouch with a lavender "A" embroidered on the front.

"What is this?" Aurora inquired. Sekhmet gestured for her to open it. Aurora did so carefully, and fine strands of auburn hair fell into Aurora's palm; a bow was attached

A Friend in Need Is a Friend Indeed

to the ends to keep them together. She stroked the small C-shaped curl. It was silky soft and dark brown with glints of red. "Is this…" Aurora's voice broke, the tears falling from her eyes.

"Her name is Angélique. I thought you might want that. I know it isn't much, but considering what you are facing, I thought this may help to remind you why you did it and encourage you to stay strong. I have one for Jarvok too, for when he's ready."

Aurora clutched the lock of hair to her chest and then kissed it. "Sekhmet, thank you. I could never repay you for all you have done," she cried.

"Please, my queen. No thanks are needed." Sekhmet's voice cracked with emotion.

"Did Jarvok read my letter?" Aurora asked, renewed hope in her voice.

"I gave it to him. The first one was confiscated by the bishops and destroyed. You were wise to write two, my queen. I gave him the second, but I could not stay to see him open it. The bishops have not left him alone for even a moment. I was lucky to get out without raising eyebrows." She shook her head.

"I am sorry you had to take such a risk for me."

Sekhmet waved her hand. "Anything for you. I am scared the next monarch will take a much harsher stance on the Court of Dark before Jarvok can read your letter, or maybe the new monarch will find out about the child before Jarvok. There are just so many things to worry about. If we had someone we could trust—" Sekhmet jumped suddenly, looking over her shoulder, as if she was startled by something. "—I think I must leave."

"Wait, Sekhmet. What about you?"

Sekhmet sat back down. "I? What do you mean?"

"What if I throw my support behind you as the next monarch? That way you can work with Jarvok to overthrow the bishops. You can protect my child until Jarvok comes to grips with everything. I won't have to worry. You are the only other one who knows about her. Once Jarvok realizes this, he can work with you to get rid of the bishops. You can rule the Court of Light, blend the two courts, and bring balance between them like we planned." Her voice was full of so much hope.

Sekhmet glanced down, trying to process the idea. "If I do this, can I stop your execution so you can be queen again?"

"No, my friend. You are sweet, but no. The bishops would know it was a ruse and take the crown away, killing both of us. I have faith in you. The sun has set on my time, but yours could be glorious." She reached for Sekhmet's hands, and the two Fae sought reassurance in each other's touch.

"My queen, I could never replace you. I don't think I can do this. No! No, I cannot." Sekhmet ripped her hands away from Aurora.

"Please, Sekhmet, I trust you. Take the crown and do wonderful things with it. Protect my child. Protect the Fae."

Sekhmet looked up at Aurora in her cell. "Yes, my queen."

Aurora shook her head. "No. You are queen now. I will tell the guards I am ready to cooperate, and I will tell the bishops I shall give my support to you as my successor, Queen Sekhmet."

Chapter Thirty-Two:
An Oath Realized

The sudden opening of the large arched doors to the left of the platform quieted the crowd. Stillness wafted through the audience of Fae as they stared at the figure in the doorway. Desdemona paused in the doorway, her shoulders squared; she looked regal. The midday sun bathed her in golden light, but her black uniform swallowed the sun's rays as if it was reminding the crowd of the sorrow and hopelessness she brought with her. She gathered her composure, though she was not afraid to face the swarm, many of whom would despise her for what she was about to do. She still had doubts she could go through with it herself. But Desdemona recognized she had no choice, even though it felt near impossible. Executing Aurora was her job and hers alone to do. It was an act of mercy and the culmination of her oath. She took a deep breath, lifted her chin, and stepped into the light, ready to do what needed to be done—what she had sworn she would do.

As expected, Desdemona was met with groans of disdain, a few cheers, and many glares. She wasn't sure if the cheers bothered her the most. She hated any of her kin who wished for Aurora's death. The wooden stairs creaked beneath her boots, and each step echoed through the crowd as her feet carried her toward the inevitable.

Desdemona surveyed the black onyx crystal pillar. They had swapped out the wooden one in case any Fae tried to use Magick or elemental power to free Aurora. She walked around and examined the mechanism that would secure Aurora, checking the ropes' tensile strength and the notches carved into the crystal meant to hold them. Only two places were scored, leaving two lengths of rope coiled on the floor of the platform, waiting like snakes for their victim.

Desdemona escaped into the icy place inside that made her so proficient as the captain of the Illuminasqua, the one with the highest kill count. She contemplated how the body would fall, based upon the ropes and their current position. These morbid details ran through her head as she determined from what angle to pierce the heart. The body would shudder backward and spasm, then lurch forward, dropping and sinking, causing a huge, unnecessary mess.

"Damn it to Lucifer, why doesn't anyone ask me before they do these things!" She was annoyed that no one had consulted the executioner when they set the pillar up. Two pillars, set three feet apart with the ropes secured at shoulder height would have allowed for less blood splattering, and her blade would have had a clean entry and exit. If the pillar was behind the body, as the setup required now, Aurora would be pinned to the pillar by the blade, making for a nasty exit. Desdemona would need to request more rope and tie Aurora at the ankles, knees, hips, waist, shoulders, and forehead to keep the body supported and upright.

An Oath Realized

Desdemona wanted Aurora to have some dignity. She motioned for the guard at the side of the platform. "You! Get me more rope!" The guard looked confused, but Desdemona reached for her blades, making one of her Harbinger grips gleam in the light. "I said to get me more rope ... now!" The guard trembled and ran off. "That's right, you better run," she said under her breath.

She preferred not to threaten the guards, but since Bishop Geddes had taken control, he had assumed authority of the Royal Guard. He had left the Illuminasqua under her command, but all the palace guards reported to the bishops now. Desdemona no longer had sway over palace security, and it was showing.

Drums sounded, and Desdemona searched for their source. The bishops were standing on the royal veranda with three drummers. "Of course they would have pageantry on such an occasion," she mumbled. Standing next to them were Zion, Asa, and King Jarvok. The thrumming of the drums was like an ominous heartbeat, a warning of what was to transpire. Everyone's attention was on the gathering of Fae above the courtyard. As her eyes scanned the occupants of the veranda, Desdemona couldn't help but ponder how times had changed.

The Dark Fae were once my comrades, then enemies, then I guess we were acquaintances, and now? I have no idea what they are except that a common enemy unites us all, according to recent events. But was Aurora the enemy? And are we a united front?

The heads of houses stopped their chattering on the smaller balconies and welcomed the bishops in their new place of power. Desdemona stood at attention, waiting for them to address her. She looked them all over one by one, saving Jarvok for last. The Dark Fae king stood in full Kyanite armor, his helmet casting a shadow over his eyes, but she could feel boring through her. They had unfinished business; one day she would clear the slate, but today was not the day.

Bishop Geddes tapped his staff on the ground four times and raised his right hand to silence the crowd of Fae. Desdemona felt it was more of a warning to keep anyone from speaking out against him. "My fellow Fae, we gather here today with heavy hearts." Groans echoed through the courtyard, and Geddes' eyes narrowed as if he were trying to see the faces of those who uttered a breath against him. He shook his head. "I know this is hard for you. It is for all of us. This has been an arduous journey, one that has led to an upsetting discovery." He bowed his head for a moment, and Desdemona felt the bile rise in her throat at his disingenuous gesture. "But today we will take the necessary step toward righting those wrongs and healing each other. Thus closing a—*hmph*—dark chapter in our history."

Zion did not miss the thinly veiled jab at the near merger of the two courts, and Geddes' clear disapproval. Nor did he appreciate it, judging by his shift in stance and Asa's hand across his stomach as he stepped forward, Desdemona noted. *It figures Geddes would insult the Dark Fae here, knowing they could not react due to the prophecy reading.* Desdemona sucked her cheeks in an attempt to cover her disapproval. *Geddes is such a coward, though that's not a surprise.*

Desdemona had never trusted Bishop Geddes, and while she had no definitive proof, she felt he somehow played a part in all of this. Desdemona was convinced there was more to this than Aurora trying to kill Jarvok due to unrest. That was not the queen she knew, though Aurora had been avoiding her for weeks. However, Desdemona could not make the puzzle pieces fit. She had tried to find proof that the bishops were plotting against the queen, but Aurora had ordered her to stop looking. She had done as she was told and now she waited to execute her queen.

The drums began to beat again, bringing her back to reality.

The large arched doors opened, and a voice called out, "Light the path toward Oblivion!"

Even though it was midday, torches were lit leading up to and surrounding the platform. Bright, blazing blue flames ignited, representing the Fae blood about to be spilled. Aurora appeared between guards Riker and Finn. For a Fae about to meet her Oblivion, she looked beautiful, regal and well, perfectly Aurora. She had been granted a bath and a fresh garment. It was a long powder-blue gown with an empire waist. There were no sleeves so she could not conceal any weapons or talismans. The gown was simple and floor length, with thin braided straps and periwinkle-blue flowers along the bust line. Her cardinal-red hair was gathered up and tied back with blue ribbon. A thick, black onyx choker was her only adornment. It was necessary to block her from calling upon her elemental Magick. Her hands were bound in the same enchanted crystal.

Desdemona's heart sank to see Aurora like this. She did not believe her queen was guilty even after all of the evidence presented. She had tried to question Aurora, digging deeper, but once Desdemona was relieved of her command of the Royal Guard, she was limited in what she could do. She felt she had failed Aurora, but she would not now.

As Aurora slowly made her way to the platform, Desdemona thought about the night of the banquet and how Aurora had looked striding down the aisle. Her queen didn't appear much different now, which Desdemona found odd. So much had changed since that night. Desdemona wished she could go back and warn herself. Aurora had started acting differently soon after, becoming more distant. Jarvok had landed here, and the bishops had launched their power play. Desdemona truly felt that if she could erase that night, things would not be like this right now.

"Captain Desdemona?" a voice shouted.

She blinked her steel grey eyes and looked up at the two guards holding Aurora.

"Is there a problem, Captain?" Bishop Geddes called down to her.

Desdemona steadied herself. "No, Bishop Geddes." She turned and accepted the prisoner from the guards. Taking the manacles from Riker, she led Aurora to the pillar in the middle of the platform. The extra rope she had requested was on the side of the pillar, and Desdemona got to work making proper use of it. She methodically moved from the bottom of Aurora's body upward, placing rope at every joint to secure her, ending at her forehead. Desdemona double-checked the manacles. As she did so, she noticed the ring Aurora wore on her right hand. It was a knuckle ring with a citrine sun and a crescent moon made of moonstone. It was Hogal's first gift to her as queen, and she had worn it every day. Desdemona remembered the day he bestowed it upon Aurora. It was her favorite.

Desdemona leaned over and whispered, "Hogal says, 'All my love and light.'" As she checked the manacles, she slipped the ring off Aurora's finger in one smooth motion and tucked it inside her vest. *Hogal would want this.*

Desdemona stepped back and examined her work. Aurora would not slump this way. Desdemona could remove the ropes and lay her down afterward to carry her to the Crystal Catacombs. Aurora gave an upturn of her lips as if to say it was okay. Desdemona could not look her in the eye. She turned toward the bishops and nodded.

On the balcony, Geddes spread his hands, his cape rippling in the breeze. "Aurora, first and only Sylph, you are hereby sentenced to meet your Oblivion for the attempted assassination of your betrothed, King Jarvok of the Court of Dark. You have confessed to your crime and waived the right to trial. You have no heir, but you have chosen to support the successor to the throne of the Court of Light, have you not?" Bishop Geddes frowned as the crowd erupted with noise.

With her forehead restrained, Aurora was limited in movement, but her voice still gave her a commanding presence. "I support the successor to the throne."

The crowd's attention was drawn back to the balcony. Bishop Geddes nodded. "I, Bishop Geddes, as the first advisor for the Court of Light, speak for all the bishops. As per Fae law, we hold the power to choose the next monarch for the Court of Light when the previous ruler has not produced an heir. We have chosen a righteous and worthy Fae: Lady Sekhmet, Head of the House of Hathor. She is of the Apolline Faction of Fae. May I present Queen Sekhmet."

With that proclamation, he stepped aside, making way as Sekhmet appeared in a simple silk gown. Sekhmet's skin had taken on a warm, rich bronze sheen, complementing the white dress. She wore a gold circlet crown with a leaf design matching her favorite giant sequoias. Her long pastel-streaked hair was braided and decorated with daisies. She came to stand at the front of the balcony.

The new queen smiled with humility as she held up a visibly shaky hand to wipe tears from her eyes. "My kin, I am humbled by Qu— Aurora's faith. I will serve you all to the best of my ability. I am sorry we must first endure tears together before we can heal. Let us not be blinded to the fact Aurora has served you well for a very long time, and while today she pays for her transgressions, never forget she brought us together." Queen Sekhmet glanced at Aurora and gave a slow blink. She dropped her chin, and a tight thin-lipped smile grew.

"Are you ready to proceed King Jarvok?" Sekhmet asked, turning to look at the Dark Fae King.

He quirked his mouth; technically, he had no qualms with Sekhmet. "Yes, but I do have one request," Jarvok said.

Chapter Thirty-Three:
REVENGE

Queen Sekhmet stood inches from King Jarvok; she was a monarch, his equal. She now faced her first real trial as queen. Jarvok's request was difficult, but well within his rights as the victim, just as Bishop Geddes had said. She had only been crowned a short time ago in a private ceremony, and the last thing she wanted to do was demonstrate weakness or upset the Court of Dark.

"I will grant your request, King Jarvok, with a caveat or favor of my own." Her melodic voice hushed the crowd.

Jarvok chuckled under his breath. "I am the victim here, Your Grace. I do not believe it is proper decorum to ask me for a favor. However, your gall has intrigued me. What is this favor that accompanies my request?" He placed his hands behind his back, a casual smirk gracing his lips.

Queen Sekhmet batted her pastel eyelashes at him. "Forgive my lack of social graces. I have been queen for all of a fruit fly's life span. No matter, my favor is simple. Please allow Bishop Geddes to give the instructions, so as not to create any ill feelings between your Fae and mine. It will help to avoid any awkwardness. I believe we both want to keep the peace between our two courts, do we not?"

Jarvok grimaced. "Well, Queen Sekhmet, it seems I have jumped to conclusions. Perhaps you are a bit more established as a leader than you appear. Of course, I will respect your request."

She nodded. "Thank you, King Jarvok. You humble me with your words." She turned toward Bishop Geddes. "Give her the instructions," she commanded.

Asa and Zion exchanged a glance. They disapproved of their king's change of plans, but to speak up now would be stupid. As if keyed into their riders' anxiety, the dragons circling above roared. The crowd and the bishops shook with fear at the beasts' outbursts. Sekhmet glanced up, and thunder rumbled in the distance. The dragons quieted down, not exactly bothered by the thunder, but they seemed to heed it as a warning.

"Perhaps we should move this along," Sekhmet said to Geddes, who was searching the sky for rainclouds. There were none to be seen.

Geddes returned his attention to his new queen. He caught the coldness in her eyes, but it lasted for but a moment. Perhaps he'd imagined it. He swallowed. "Yes, Your Grace, right away." He walked toward the railing. "Captain Desdemona, are you prepared to carry out your orders?"

Desdemona stood at attention and gave a quick bow. "I am." She unsheathed her Elestial Blade and held it up for Geddes to see. The crowd had one of two reactions; they either oohed and ahhed at the glow of the Auric sword blazing from her right forearm, or they wept at the sight of it, knowing what it would be used for.

Revenge

"Captain, there has been a slight change of plans," Bishop Geddes said, sending a flicker of hope through Desdemona as the crowd broke out into chatter. But she knew the bishops all too well; she braced for what was to come next.

"The first strike will be with the Elestial Blade, making Aurora susceptible to the instrument of her Oblivion: the Harbinger swords," Bishop Geddes said, his voice lacking the authoritative quality it once had.

The crowd erupted into an incoherent mixture of screams and sobs, along with other undecipherable tones. Desdemona felt her rage boil. It licked at the inside of her skin, begging to be released. Her hands twitched toward her swords. She could easily take them all on. She stared at Jarvok, knowing this was his idea, his revenge. Many had described rage as something cold, but not hers—Desdemona's fury was hot. It was an equal-opportunity anger, destroying everything in its path, leaving nothing but ashes. Jarvok may have survived crashing back to Earth, but her fire was all-consuming and burned through hope and love. No Fae survived that, and one day he would know it.

"So be it," Desdemona said through gritted teeth.

Up on the veranda with King Jarvok, Asa stumbled back, breaking out in a sweat. The king's gaze slid toward his seer before returning his attention toward his former betrothed. He rubbed his chin, hiding his viper smile.

Zion steadied her. "What the hell was that?"

Asa swallowed, her breathing ragged. "I have never felt anger like that from another except Him."

Zion stared at Desdemona. "You don't mean..." He wiped Asa's chin as the sweat dripped from her face.

"Yes, I do." The two stared at their former comrade with newfound fear.

Desdemona faced Aurora, her eyes blurring already with unshed tears. Aurora's eyes only conveyed empathy and love, which made this much harder.

"Loyalty to the kin…" Aurora reminded her in a soft voice.

Desdemona lined up her Elestial Blade with Aurora's sternum, the fabric from the blue gown already sizzling from inches away. She braced her left hand on Aurora's right shoulder and pulled her fist back by her ear.

"Not to the crown." Desdemona finished the oath as she drove the blade into her queen, purposely missing her heart. The crunch of bone was deafening; the crowd screamed and gasped, but Desdemona was already in her dark place. The fire raged in her heart, and all she could hear was white noise. The world was still. She watched as the light in Aurora's eyes flickered, the regal monarch fading and the scared Fae revealing herself with each struggling pump of her heart. Desdemona retracted her Auric blade, Aurora's blood evaporated from the heat of it.

Desdemona reached into her boots for her Harbinger swords. She circled her wrists, and the swords readied themselves, their gleaming hooked blades ready to deliver death. She laid the right blade on her forehead in a show of respect before her kill, with the left grip over her heart, the blade pointing downward. She crossed her wrists and struck her blades downward—ready.

The entry wound was small, as the heat from her Elestial Blade had curtailed most of the mess. However, the blood had to go somewhere, and Aurora coughed, blue liquid spattering from her lips. Desdemona wiped it away

Revenge

from Aurora's mouth with her thumb and index finger. "It will be over now," she said softly to her friend and queen. She lined up the swords, one at the top of the heart and one just below, hooks pointed up and down. Desdemona wanted to be sure the heart would be shredded so it could not be used in any Magick. She drew back the swords, and Aurora gave a strained tip of her chin. "Never to the crown again, only to my kin," Desdemona whispered.

The captain took a crane stance, her right knee tucked up high, back straight, chin raised, blades pointed at her target, and circled the swords past her hips in a fluid motion. Then, she brought the swords back up and dropped her weight onto her front foot in a deep lunge. This caused her to drive the blades with the utmost force she could muster into Aurora's chest, whose screams abruptly cut off as the swords plunged deeply into her body. Desdemona did not stop pushing until the blades stuck out of the back of the black onyx pillar, buried up to the hilt in Aurora's chest wall.

A flash of blue light glowed and then suffused to shades of pink. Aurora's energy wings manifested one last time. Her body jerked on the pole, her back arching with this final ethereal display of power. The ropes strained like they were trying to contain both the energy and the body, but Desdemona steadied Aurora until she stilled. Desdemona thought she saw the pink wings turn gold and feathery before they vanished, but she couldn't be sure with all that was going on.

With Aurora impaled upon the Harbinger blades, she managed to whisper something to Desdemona with her last strangled breath. The captain's eyes grew wide. Inches apart, Desdemona watched as Aurora's turquoise eyes closed and her mouth went slack. Then, with a sickening wet pop, Desdemona wrenched her Harbinger swords from Aurora's chest cavity and backed up as the blood pooled upon the platform.

Desdemona's job was done. Her former queen and first true friend was dead by her Harbinger swords.

Phew! This was a doozy, my Fae friends. Grab a box of tissues and maybe some plum sugar wine and meet me back in the Veil, because there is a lot to unpack coming up in book five of the *Birth of the Fae* series: *A Fae is Done*. King Jarvok will return shortly, as will the new queen of the Court of Light, Queen Sekhmet, and well, most of the Fae. As always, let me know your thoughts on Instagram @Birthofthefae_novel or on Twitter @ Birthofthefae. You can also visit my website for all things Fae: BirthoftheFae.com.

Chaos be with you,
~Danielle

4 Horsemen Publications

Romance

Ann Shepphird
The War Council

Emily Bunney
All or Nothing
All the Way
All Night Long: Novella
All She Needs
Having it All
All at Once
All Together
All for Her

Lynn Chantale
The Baker's Touch
Blind Secrets
Broken Lens

Mimi Francis
Private Lives
Private Protection
Run Away Home
The Professor

Fantasy, SciFi, & Paranormal Romance

Beau Lake
The Beast Beside Me
The Beast Within Me
Taming the Beast: Novella
The Beast After Me
Charming the Beast: Novella
The Beast Like Me
An Eye for Emeralds
Swimming in Sapphires
Pining for Pearls

King
Traitor
His Last Name

J.M. Paquette
Klauden's Ring
Solyn's Body
The Inbetween
Hannah's Heart
Call Me Forth
Invite Me In
Keep Me Close

D. Lambert
To Walk into the Sands
Rydan
Celebrant
Northlander
Esparan

Lyra R. Saenz
Prelude
Falsetto in the Woods: Novella

Ragtime Swing
Sonata
Song of the Sea
The Devil's Trill
Bercuese
To Heal a Songbird
Ghost March
Nocturne

Sessrúmnir

VALERIE WILLIS
Cedric: The Demonic Knight
Romasanta: Father of Werewolves
The Oracle: Keeper of the Gaea's Gate
Artemis: Eye of Gaea
King Incubus: A New Reign

T.S. SIMONS
Antipodes
The Liminal Space
Ouroboros
Caim

V.C. WILLIS
Prince's Priest
Priest's Assassin

YOUNG ADULT FANTASY

BLAISE RAMSAY
Through The Black Mirror
The City of Nightmares
The Astral Tower
The Lost Book of the Old Blood
Shadow of the Dark Witch
Chamber of the Dead God

Broken Beginnings: Story of Thane
Shattered Start: Story of Sera
Sins of The Father: Story of Silas
Honorable Darkness: Story of Hex and Snip
A Love Lost: Story of Radnar

C.R. RICE
Denial
Anger
Bargaining
Depression
Acceptance

VALERIE WILLIS
Rebirth
Judgment
Death

4HORSEMENPUBLICATIONS.COM